THE KEEPING PLACE

THE WITCH HUNTER SAGA - BOOK SIX

NICOLE R. TAYLOR

Chapter 1

Nye Saer stared into the empty fireplace and screwed up his nose.

He'd rarely felt tired in his four hundred and twenty something years as a vampire, but being the leader of the London vampires was beginning to grate. Big time. That and the events of the last few months.

Crazy ex-girlfriends with epic revenge plots would be the death of him...and he was already technically dead as a doornail and then some.

It hadn't even been a week since he'd been torn from the clutches of the Unhallowed, the ragtag group of witches turned wraiths led by his ex-girlfriend Eleanor. They'd carved a symbol into his chest as part of their screwed-up ritual to tie him to the ley lines. Without his vampirism, they would have needed to refresh their conduit time and time again, but with his ability to heal himself, they'd had a constant connection to the earth and an unlimited stream of power...not to mention leaving him in agony twenty-four seven.

It was a totally screwed-up revenge plot if you asked him, but he'd sacrificed himself to save Isobel from a terrible curse.

Isobel. At the thought of the fiery haired human, his heart softened. He would have suffered millennia so she could have lived a handful of happy, healthy years.

The door opened behind him, and he turned to find the witch Gabby Cohen slinking into the study. The Hampstead mansion where they now resided was hers, gifted to her after the death of the last original founding vampire, the two-thousand-year-old Roman, Regulus, who was also the last leader of the London vampires. That was another long story.

Her olive complexion, dark chestnut hair, and brown eyes were a familiar sight by now. They'd fought many foes together over the last year and suffered many losses. They were firm allies, but sometimes, he wasn't sure they were friends...not yet. The whole witches versus vampire thing got muddy now and then. Nye knew she would choose her own kind without hesitation if it ever came down to it.

"How's your chest?" Gabby asked, eyeing him in that judgmental way she had. "Any residual effects?"

His thoughts shifted from Isobel to the rune Eleanor had carved into his chest, the rune that had taken longer than it should to heal after the connection to the ley line was severed, and he began to feel uneasy. Something felt different about him, he was sure of it, but he couldn't quite work out what. The mark had faded completely given enough time, but in his imagination, it still lingered. He rubbed at the phantom itch and rolled his eyes.

"You need to get it together," Gabby said.

"I need to get it together?" he exclaimed, turning to face her fully. "Have you seen Tristan lately? He's this close to crying into his cereal." He held up his forefinger and thumb, pinching them together. "Don't tell me what I should do, Gabby."

Ever since Tristan had the compulsion Eleanor had unknowingly cast on him, the thousand-year-old knight had been sulking. Honestly, it pissed Nye off. More than ever, he needed all hands on deck to face the threat of the Unhallowed. Doubt and depression would see them all dead.

"You're not the only one with problems, Nye, and your inaction is beginning to worry me. Eleanor is still out there if you haven't forgotten."

"How could I," he muttered, a vision of the wraith's look of rage as he'd plunged her knife into his chest, severing her connection to the ley lines. He'd forgotten a lot of things in his long life, but the moment the steel had sliced into his flesh and the flow of power ceased... well, he would never forget that.

"I don't know what you want me to do, Gabby," he went on. "You said it yourself. Wraiths weren't meant to exist anymore. They haven't been seen for at least a thousand years. No one knows how to end them or even where they went after you blasted them with your power."

She sank into one of the armchairs by the dark fireplace and sighed, giving away how strung out she really was. She was the most powerful witch currently walking the earth, and he knew it had taken more than he could fathom to overwhelm the wraiths the night of the ritual.

Considering the energy that was in her grasp, even she didn't have enough in her to end them for good.

Gabby remained silent. Even she didn't know the answers to her annoying questions, and she was a walking witchy almanac. That was it then. They were as good as doomed, and all they were currently doing was buying time.

"We are all weak," Nye said, casting away his thoughts of their terminal status. "The last thing we need is for that news to get out. We must show a united front and let the vampires think the Unhallowed have been dealt with. A revolt now would be bad."

"You don't have to tell me," was her reply. "I can't even light a candle. Thank goodness the wards around the manor are still intact."

"Then we buy time. Enjoy our last days of freedom."

"You're giving up?" she asked incredulously. "Nye—"

"What other recourse do we have?" he snapped, interrupting her. "I don't know about you, but our end is coming. Not today, not tomorrow, or maybe in a hundred years, but it is coming."

"How very Sylvia Plath of you," Gabby retorted. "We all have an expiration date, Nye, even you. Nothing can live forever but damned if I'm going to let our end be at the hands of the Unhallowed. Don't be so quick to give up. Isobel sure hasn't."

At the mention of Isobel's name, he ground his teeth together. The feeling of helplessness he'd been suffering ever since he'd been dragged away from that stone circle was threatening to drown him completely. There was no way to fight them...

"So what now, Gabby?" he asked, turning to stare at her. "If there is hope, tell me now. What's your plan?"

She stared at him, her eyes full of fierce rage. "First, we regain our strength. Then we find any information about their kind, no matter the cost of getting it. Once we are armed, we wait and watch. Finally, when she comes, we'll be ready for her."

He snorted. She'd obviously been thinking about it a great deal while he sulked alongside Tristan.

Gabby's plan seemed simple, but with their lives in the balance, it was more difficult than anything. Where would they look? Who could they turn to? He had absolutely no idea, and neither did she.

Casting out his hearing, Nye heard the faint pitter-patter of Isobel's heartbeat and the thumps as she stormed around the bathroom, attempting to fix his handiwork on the marble basin. She was a human being, fragile, yet her mind was stronger than any vampire he'd ever known. She was intelligent beyond compare, her resolve impenetrable. Isobel had no way of fighting the Unhallowed, yet she'd stood up to Eleanor, anyway.

Nye had thought he'd seen it all, but the day he'd opened his eyes and saw her...*damn*. Who would've thought a human with barely three decades on her could have so much to teach a vampire with four centuries under his belt? Not him, that was certain.

"Go," Gabby said, watching him closely. "Be with her. She needs you, but I think you need her more."

Rolling his eyes, Nye left the study in search of Isobel, cursing under his breath. *Damn witches.*

Isobel stared at the cracked marble basin in her bathroom and sighed.

Nye had broken it the other day. He'd been in a rage after she and her friends had rescued him from that crazy Unhallowed ritual at the standing stones outside of London. Knowing he had vampire super-strength, Isobel knew his anger had been restrained. If he could crack a solid piece of marble with his bare hands, she imagined what he could do when he didn't hold himself back. She shook her head, feeling tired.

She was nothing but a frail human being in a sea of supernatural creatures far superior to her. Talk about in over her head.

Ever since her best friend, the witch Gabby, had sent the Unhallowed packing, Isobel had been tired. Worried the curse Eleanor had put on her had come back—after Nye had sacrificed himself to save her from it—she'd fretted, but she hadn't fallen to the lethargy she'd experienced before. Putting it down to stress, she turned to her reflection and dragged a comb through her fiery hair. She was a little dark around her eyes.

Surely, it was stress from the lingering threat of Eleanor and her squad of freaky wraiths. Her newly acquired vampire boyfriend wasn't helping with his perpetual moodiness either.

Oh, Nye, she thought to herself. Why did she always have to be attracted to the bad boys? The chase was thrilling, but the reality of a relationship was a much different basket of fruit.

Isobel stared at herself in the mirror for a moment longer and sighed. Being depressed over her fragility would do her no good. It was a fact, and that was that. She just had to suck it up and deal.

A shadow appeared in the mirror over her shoulder, and she yelped as the shape of a man hovered in the background. Realising the apparition was her brother Alex, she spun on her heel.

"Alex!" she practically screeched, holding her hand over her pounding heart. "Don't do that!"

"Sorry," her brother said sheepishly. "I'm still getting used to the whole sound barrier thing. I keep breaking it and not realising."

Snorting, Isobel turned and flicked off the bathroom light, plunging the room into darkness. One day, she would come to terms with the fact her little brother was a truly immortal vampire. Nothing but their friend Aya, the vampire Celestine hybrid, could put an end to him. He was still within the first year of his transition and was constantly forgetting his own strength...and hunger.

"How are you feeling?" he asked, ushering her to sit on the couch out in the bedroom.

The fancy room Nye had installed Isobel in all that time ago had fast become home, despite her annoyance at being held hostage—it had been for her own protection, or so he said. It was a small apartment in itself with a king-sized bed donned in silk sheets, a leather couch and armchair set, an open fireplace, an enormous television, and a black marble bathroom complete with pearly bathtub with golden, clawed feet. The only thing missing was its own little kitchenette and butler.

Isobel flopped down on the couch and stretched out her legs as her brother took one of the armchairs. It didn't escape her notice that his eye had wandered and taken in all of Nye's discarded clothing on the floor. It wasn't a secret he disapproved of the budding relationship she was sharing with the four-hundred-year-old spy. But he was genuinely trying to remain calm, so she'd give him points for that.

"I'm okay," she replied. "I'm tired, but it's nothing to do with the curse. I'm normal human tired."

"Good," Alex said. "Has Nye been treating you okay? Because if he hasn't, you know I'm stronger than he is. I can snap him in half." He held up his hands. "Just say the word."

She laughed and nudged him with her foot. "Don't scare him off just yet, okay?"

He smiled, but it seemed to fade faster than it had appeared. "I'm worried, Iz."

Thinking about the lingering threat of the Unhallowed wraiths, she shrugged. "Yeah, well, there's not much we can do about that."

"I can't help but feel we're on borrowed time," he said, his brow furrowing. "Are you really sure you want to stay? We can go someplace far away, and I can protect you. Staying here..."

Isobel shook her head, squashing down the irritation Alex's words had invoked. "No," was her declaration. "I can't leave him, Alex. I'm sure there's something I can do to help. No one knows anything about wraiths or the history behind the Unhallowed. I've worked my whole life to understand the ancient people and cultures of the world. Not to mention all their myths. I have access to one of the greatest libraries and depositories of ancient texts in the world at Oxford University. I have contacts. Albeit, they may not be supernatural, but we found Katrin's grimoire in the vault there, didn't we? Who knows what else is in there. If there's a chance I can uncover something, no matter how small, then I'm going to stay."

"For him?" was Alex's reply.

"For Nye, yes, but not just him. For everyone." She shuffled along the couch so she could reach out for her brother's hand, which she took in her own. His skin was so cold to the touch these days. "Alex, you have to trust me. And if you can't trust me, trust Gabby. We'll find a way to fight the Unhallowed. I'm sure of it."

Alex stared at her for a moment, and she hoped some of her conviction would rub off on him. He might be immortal, but she would always be older, that was, until the day she died, and he went on. Older meant wiser, right?

"I'm not going anywhere anytime soon," he said after a moment.

"Thanks, little brother. I don't know if I could do any of this without you."

"Am I interrupting?"

Isobel glanced up at the sound of Nye's voice and smiled. Standing at barely five foot eight with a twisted scar running diagonally across his face and his unkempt hair, the vampire looked more like a back alley thief than a powerful leader.

"Nye," she said, her heart fluttering. "Not at all."

His lips quirked, and she knew he'd heard the skip in her steady pulse, which meant Alex had, too.

"I think that's my signal," her brother said wryly, getting up out of the armchair.

Wanting some alone time with Nye, she allowed Alex to leave, but she wouldn't have been able to say so otherwise. He'd just evaporated, darting from the room faster than her gaze could follow.

Nye hadn't even acknowledged the founder, his sights still firmly fixed on Isobel. Stepping forward, he sat beside her and opened his arms, scooping her close. Touching seemed to be coming easier to the vampire. His small endearments—a stroke of the cheek, an embrace, a chaste kiss—were becoming more frequent. She couldn't blame him for taking things slowly. There was that time when he lost control and got all randy and bit her in a fit of passion.

"Are you well?" he asked, breathing deeply.

"I'm okay," she replied, melting into his touch.

He looked at her pointedly, his gaze searching her features.

"*Nye.*"

"Fine," he said. "What do you want to do tonight?"

"Tonight?" was her confused reply. "Don't you have any diabolical vampire shenanigans to attend to?"

He smirked. "Diabolical vampire shenanigans?"

"Oh, you know what I mean."

"No," he said. "I'm all yours tonight. I know we

haven't spent much time together since..." he trailed off, a frown creasing his pale forehead.

She wasn't a fool. She knew the rune Eleanor had carved into his chest still bothered him. Honestly, it still worried her, too.

"Whatever you like," she said.

"How about I answer some of your questions. For your thesis."

She pulled back and stared up at him in surprise. "Really? I thought you didn't—"

"Take the offer while it's good, Isobel," he interrupted.

Thrilled that Nye actually wanted to talk about the parts of his human life he remembered, she placed a soft kiss on his lips. "Let me just get my notes."

Maybe it was foolish, or maybe it was a mere distraction, but she still hoped she could pick up the tattered remains of her life and go back to the Master's program at Oxford University. The life she'd been plucked from the day she decided to check up on Alex and had been imprisoned by Nye instead. Finishing her thesis was important to her even though it might not amount to anything considering their vermin problem.

Snatching up her notebooks and laptop, she flung herself down on the bed and patted the space beside her, which Nye took.

"Get comfortable," she said with a wicked smile. "I've got a lot of questions."

Chapter 2

Gabby lingered in the study long after Nye left to be with Isobel.

Her thoughts drifted to the task at hand, and her anxiety began to rise at the unknown path they must take to face the Unhallowed. Nye had declared his lack of faith, but she was far from ready to resign herself to being syphoned until she was nothing but a withered husk.

Piecing together what she knew, she tried to make sense of the mystery.

The night of the ritual at the standing stones, she'd stepped into the ether and allowed her spirit to soak in the waning power of the ley lines, desperate for any clue to help her against the wraiths. The ancestor spirits had guided her, showing her a vision of the moment Nye had ended Eleanor's human life back in the early sixteen hundreds. The wraith had attacked the spy and attempted to carve a symbol in his forehead, marking him for something unknown. Had it been the same symbol she'd used the night of the ritual? She'd been shoved into Eleanor's body to witness the scene but wasn't privy to her intent. It could have been anything.

Speaking of being inside that bitch's body... She'd seen, heard, and felt everything that point in time had to offer, including the moment Eleanor pressed up against her friend—for lack of a better word to describe him—and shoved her tongue down his throat. It was a bit too much information. Since then, she'd had a hard time looking at Nye without thinking about the kiss. Puke.

Still, something the spirits revealed to her had her on edge.

Her mother, the last matriarch of the Unhallowed, had bidden Eleanor to bear the fruit of their salvation. What did that mean? And what did carving a rune into Nye have to do with it? What was so special about him they'd waited over four hundred years to strike? It couldn't just be revenge, not after what Tristan had told her while he was still under Eleanor's control. Then there was the matter of the Keeping Place. It seemed to hold something they needed.

Anyway, their end goal was simple. Eleanor wanted to resurrect the Unhallowed. *All of them.*

If Gabby never worked out what all those things meant, she wouldn't understand how to stop Eleanor from reanimating her army of dark witches. A whole coven of wraiths and their tainted spirit magic unleashed on the world was bad news. More than bad news...it was *headline news*. How long would it be before they went on a rampage and began siphoning and sacrificing innocent humans? Not long at all.

There was a soft knock at the door, and she turned to find Reed hovering just outside.

"Are you ready to go?" the vampire asked, raising an eyebrow. "You look like you're about to throw up."

Reed was a new addition to the team, employed by Nye as a member of the new incarnation of the Six, and he'd fast proved his loyalty and worth. So much so, she'd invited him to come inside the manor.

Still, he was largely an unknown quantity. She didn't even know how old he was. Outward appearance was not an indicator of a vampire's age. Regulus hadn't looked a day over thirty, but he had been over two thousand. At the thought of her lost love, she closed her eyes and shook her head.

"I'm fine," she replied briskly. "I've just got a lot on my mind."

He nodded but didn't reply. All he did was wait calmly for her to collect her things and make a move.

In the wake of the ritual and her depleted powers, Gabby had ditched the human driver employed by Regulus and chosen a hardier employee—Reed—to take over her chauffeuring needs in the wake of their recent adventures. The vampire hardly looked the part in his black skinny jeans, boots, fitted T-shirt, and shirt opened at the collar. He looked like a bad boy greaser from the nineteen sixties. All that was missing was the hotrod with the flames painted on the hood.

Downstairs in the garage, he opened the back door to the sleek black sedan and waved her inside. Taking the front, he pressed the fob to open the roller door.

Finally, he glanced at her in the rearview mirror and asked, "Where to, ma'am?" Then he shot her a cheeky wink.

Hiding a smile, she fired her answer directly into his mind, *Fulham Palace Road, Hammersmith.*

"Geesus!" he cursed, almost jumping out of his skin.

"Sorry, did I tickle you a bit?"

"Dammit," he exclaimed, starting the car. "I thought you were on mute."

"I guess I'm charging up faster than I anticipated."

"I'll say," he muttered as they pulled out onto the road and began their journey through the darkening streets of London.

Gabby watched the side of Reed's face as he navigated the lingering peak hour traffic and wondered about him. He'd been extremely helpful throughout the whole Unhallowed debacle, and until Nye had plucked him from obscurity to become part of the Six, he'd never crossed her radar. All the vampires she'd known had turbulent pasts, and she wondered if his was the same.

"Where did you come from, anyway?" she asked rather suddenly.

Reed chuckled softy, giving away that he knew she'd been staring at him. "You get straight to the point, don't you? Right to the crux of a vampire's most personal experience."

She shrugged as he flickered a glance at her in the mirror.

"How did you lose your virginity?" he asked abruptly, raising an eyebrow.

Knowing he was trying to make her feel uneasy, she shrugged again. "Jake Harrington. One-night stand when I was eighteen. It was terrible, and I never got a single thing out if it, if you know what I'm saying." She held up her hand and wiggled her little finger. "Little, limp, and premature."

Reed laughed, a full and hearty peal that had her smiling. "I like you," he declared as he turned a corner. "You're such an unashamed thing."

"So where did you come from?" she asked again.

"I was a soldier before," he replied, tipping his imaginary hat. "Cattle class."

"Infantry?"

"Like I said, *cattle class*."

Knowing there was a story behind his jovial attitude toward his past, she shook her head and let him be. Knowing how war had negatively affected her friend Zac Degaud, she knew pressing would do neither of them any good.

"How old are you, then?"

"Twenty-seven. Have been for a while now."

Laughing at his blatant avoidance, she let him have that one. He'd tell her the story if he wanted to and not a moment before. *Damn vampires.*

The ride over to Hammersmith was smooth. Pushing away thoughts of the Unhallowed, for the time being, she pondered another pressing matter. This one, she actually had a lead on and was the very thing that had led her to an unassuming little block of flats by a flyover in the western part of London.

Yesterday, Isobel had mentioned to her she'd been tired but had put it down to plain human failings such as not enough sleep and stress. Unfortunately, Gabby could see things a little more clearly than most, and her sight told her the curse Eleanor had wrought had left its mark. If the wraith came back, it wouldn't take much for her to reinstate it. She wouldn't even have to be in the same room to focus her will on Izzy. It was just another item on the list of bad things that could happen anytime from now to a hundred years away.

Gabby was determined to be ready to counter the curse next time, though she hoped she wouldn't have to. Preparation was nine-tenths of the law, after all.

Reed parked the car in the clearway outside the redbrick Tudor-style building and turned to face her. "Do you want me to wait? I can't park here, but I can leave this beast around the corner and watch from afar."

"Keep hidden," she said, easing herself from the car. "Last thing we need is to announce our presence."

He nodded and waited, letting the car idle as she closed the door and approached the entrance to the flat. Thankful he was lingering until she was well and truly inside, she raised her hand and knocked.

A second later, the door swung open, and an elderly lady appeared, her stature tiny compared to her own. Her white hair was cropped short, a cream blouse hung from her bony shoulders, a paisley skirt flowed past her knees, and her legs were covered in beige pantyhose while her feet were stuck in a pair of fluffy pink slippers. The woman's skin might have been withered, but her eyes were sharp as an eagle's as they passed over the witch on her doorstep.

"So that's what you look like," the woman said, squinting at Gabby. "A little younger than I presumed, but no one can tell these days."

Gabby cocked an eyebrow.

"Plastic surgery, dear," she said with a chuckle, her voice whistling a little. "Who's got the time or energy to maintain a web of youth when the world is full of disgusting creatures?" She peered over Gabby's shoulder at the car and scowled. "You can come in, but leave your...whatever it is...outside."

She nodded. "That's why I left him there. As you said, foul things are afoot, and it pays to have a hardy driver at one's disposal."

The woman smiled and waved her inside. "Come

in then, dear. Do you like scones? I have a brand-new jar of raspberry jam from the church farmer's market if you'd like to try some. They have a darling little stall. I get a new flavour the first Saturday of every month."

Gabby frowned at the juxtaposition of the lady before her but stepped into the house without hesitation. The door was closed behind her with a hearty slam, and she turned to face the woman.

"Now that he's shut out, I can introduce myself. I'm Gloria. Earth witch, going on eighty-eight years...or so I tell people."

"How long have you been eighty-eight?" she asked as she was lead into the witch's home.

"A while, but they never remember." Gloria giggled as she turned to her little kitchenette and put the kettle on. "Have a seat, dear, I'll be right with you."

While the elderly witch busied herself readying her spread of tea and scones, Gabby turned to the brightly lit flat. She didn't know what she was expecting to see, but it wasn't the wall of herbs, crystals, and grimoires her imagination had conjured. Before her was floral wallpaper, a mahogany and glass buffet full of porcelain figures of draft horses, a floral settee with a crocheted rug set on the back, various landscape paintings on the walls, a sepia portrait of a man in military uniform, and lace curtains adorning the windows. The kitchen was suitably bright and floral to match, and commemorative plates featuring various British royal family weddings were lined up over the little dining table.

Gently nudging the curtain aside, Gabby peered out of the window and saw the church sitting directly next door, not ten meters from where she now stood. Wondering if a ley line passed through it, she began to feel uneasy. Not all holy sites sat upon one, but she didn't have the ability to sense out the earth power unless she was standing directly above it.

"St. Augustine's," Gloria said, nodding toward the window as she set down a tray laden with scones, jam, a little bowl of cream, a dish of sugar cubes, a teapot, and cups and saucers. She had a great deal of strength in her for her age, but Gabby knew better. Magic was in play.

"I like living close to holy ground," Gloria went on. "Though most of the land here is concrete and cobblestones. There isn't much soil nowadays."

"How long have you lived here?" Gabby asked, allowing the curtain to flutter back into place.

"Oh, more years than I care to remember. I'm a fixture I'm afraid." She sat gingerly in a well-worn armchair as Gabby perched gingerly on the settee. "Now, Gabrielle Cohen, shall we get down to business, or can I chastise you for scaring me half to death when you contacted me?"

She shifted nervously, knowing she'd given the witch a fright when she'd requested a meeting, not through a telephone call but a method much more fitting for witchy coercion. Telepathy and astral projection.

"I apologise for being rude," she said. "There are many forces that wish me harm. I had to be sure. Frankly, I was surprised you knew who I was."

Gloria pursed her lips. "Dear, everyone knows who you are." She busied herself with the tray, then offered a plate to the young witch. "Scone?"

Taking the floral china from her gnarled fingers, Gabby smiled, totally thrown by Gloria's sudden change back to a sweet little old lady. "Thank you."

Pleased that she'd taken the scone, Gloria poured herself some tea. "Now I know there's more to your story than you care to tell me. Most powerful witch alive, affinity with the ether, vampire lover, hybrid hunter, etcetera, etcetera... Nobody comes to see an old bat like me without wanting something."

"I was told you have a rather specific specialisation," Gabby replied, getting straight to the point. Since her reputation had preceded her, there was no use attempting to be anything but direct.

Gloria sipped at her tea, then replied, "I do, much to my detriment it seems."

"Do you know anything that could counteract a degenerative curse?"

"A curse? Well..."

"That's your specialisation, isn't it?" Gabby raised her eyebrow. "I'm not here to render punishment, Gloria, if that's why you're sidestepping. I need help."

"Ah, perhaps." She set down her cup and saucer. "There are few people who come to see me with noble intentions. I had to be sure, also. Who do you want cursed?"

"No, I don't want to curse anyone," she exclaimed. "I want to know if a curse can be *removed*."

Gloria snorted and shook her head. "No one can stop a curse once it's latched on."

Her heart began to sink. If there was no way to stop Eleanor from reigniting the poison she'd placed inside Isobel, then was her friend doomed no matter what she did? The wraith was so spiteful that Gabby knew the moment she siphoned enough energy to regain her human form, she'd go straight for Izzy. If the markers the curse had left behind couldn't be removed, then there had to be a way to shield her.

"I have a friend," Gabby began uneasily. "She was cursed with a degenerative spell, a black poison that threatened to drown her. It was lifted, but..."

"Its markers remain," the old witch finished for her.

She nodded. "Is there any way to help her? Can the markers be removed?"

Gloria looked grave as she thought over Gabby's question. "I know a way you might be able to put a stopper on it, but it wouldn't remove the curse entirely. Whoever bears the poison will carry it the rest of their lives. Is your intent truly noble, dear?"

"I don't know what you've heard about me, but everything I've ever done was to save lives."

"What about your vampire friends?"

"That's a grey area, I admit it, but not all vampires are inherently evil. There are witches who have turned to darkness just as there are those who have remained in the light." She raised an eyebrow at the elderly witch. "Then there are those with feet on both sides. We are not immune, and neither are vampires."

Gloria sighed and rolled her eyes. Gesturing for Gabby to wait, she pushed herself up from the armchair with a groan. "Wait here," she said. "I have the exact thing you need."

Chapter 3

That night, Nye remained awake with Isobel, attempting to answer her thousand and one questions about a life he scarcely cared to remember.

The Middle Ages hadn't been all sunshine and roses considering he'd been dragged up kicking and screaming in London's slums. Some childhood. Still, that life had shaped him dramatically, and a vampire always remembered their most defining moments... much to his detriment.

Isobel wanted to complete her thesis, and he wanted to distract her from the inevitable end. How could he tell her there was no hope? How could he break her heart? He couldn't, so he humoured her.

A new day dawned over the city, and as Isobel slept, he listened to the hushed sounds of the manor. With only him, Tristan, Gabby, Alex, and the comings and goings of Reed and the Six, the place was quiet. After such turmoil, it made him feel uneasy. Like they were living through the calm before the storm.

His ears tingled at the sound of rustling coming from the direction of the study and then a soft cough. Gabby. Glancing at Isobel, he smoothed a strand of brilliant hair from her forehead and traced her cheek. He'd allow her to sleep a few more hours.

Sliding off the bed, he gently picked up her notebooks and laptop, setting them in a neat pile on the bedside table. Finally, he adjusted the quilt over her before ghosting from the room.

Down the hall, the door to the study was closed.

Opening it, he found Gabby sitting on the floor among a pile of grimoires, her own open in her lap, her fingers speckled with ink. It seemed she'd been concocting something witchy while he regaled Isobel with stories of his dreary past life.

"Where'd you go last night?" he asked her, closing the door behind him. "I hope Reed behaved himself."

"You don't have to worry about Reed," the witch replied, not even glancing up from her work. "You chose well with that one."

"I know."

She glanced up and laughed softly. "What about you? Where'd you go last night? You're wearing the same clothes."

"Nowhere," he replied, sitting in one of the armchairs by the empty fireplace. "I stayed up with Isobel. She wanted to ask me questions for her thesis, so I humoured her. She still thinks she's going back to her studies."

Gabby frowned and closed her grimoire with a snap. "There's still a chance she can, you know. I know you're being a Negative Nancy, Nye, but don't suck the hope from everyone else. Especially Izzy."

Perhaps she was right, but his mind hadn't changed since their last conversation.

"So where'd you go?" he prodded.

"I went to see a contact," was her brisk reply. "Unlike you, I'm still chipping away at our pest problem."

Nye grunted.

"Have you seen Tristan this morning?"

"He's still hiding away," he replied. "I haven't seen the ugly bastard since you dragged him back from the stone circle."

"Give him some time, Nye."

"It's cowardly."

"Hypocrite," she replied. "You can't blame him after what Eleanor made him do against his will. Loyalty is important to him. More so than it is to you. The fact he was compelled cut him deep. It violated something he holds sacred. It'll take time for him to come to terms with it."

He waved a hand at her, not wanting to talk about the knight a moment longer. He'd all but abandoned them as far as he was concerned. Yeah, he was a hypocrite, so what? At least he hadn't resorted to hiding.

"Did you find out anything from your contact, then?" he asked, nodding at the pile of grimoires.

"I did want to discuss something with you," Gabby began, rising to her feet and taking the chair opposite his.

He grunted and leaned back, rubbing his temples. Great, another question and answer session. Isobel was lucky he loved her. He'd bend over backward and suffer an eternity of excruciating pain for that woman, but Gabby... Well, he could take it or leave it.

"So..." she began uneasily. "I had a vision the other night."

His gaze flickered to hers with interest. "What vision?"

"When I stayed behind at the stone circle," she began. "The spirits showed me you and Eleanor..."

Nye narrowed his eyes, pretty damn sure where this was going already. "Go on..."

She eyed him uneasily. "When you cut off her head."

Shit. He'd recalled that day more times than he wanted to in recent weeks and having Gabby witness it firsthand? He was ashamed that she'd seen him at his most vulnerable. In love with a witch who was turned against him, who he then had to kill in order to save his own wretched life. That meant Gabby and seen the moment Regulus had shown up and claimed his servitude.

Regulus. *Her* dearly departed love.

"Why are you bringing this up?" he asked stonily, too exhausted to care for the witch's feelings.

"The spirits never meddle unless they have something worth saying." Her fingers tightened around the arm of the chair, making the leather creak. She was...embarrassed?

"So why are you hesitating? Just tell me what you saw."

"I was in the memory...as Eleanor."

"You were..." He suddenly began to realise why she was a little flushed. That day, Eleanor had...

Gabby nodded.

"You kissed me as Eleanor?" he asked, raising his eyebrows.

"I was totally grossed out, by the way, so don't go thinking I'm going to try to dry hump your leg or anything."

"Good," he said, an amused smile playing at his lips. "Isobel would tear you apart."

"Cocky son of a—"

"Calm your farm," he interrupted. "You brought up my most embarrassing moment for a reason. Why did your spooky mates show it to you? So you could torture me with it? Is this their version of a ghostly beyond the grave prank?"

Gabby smiled, her shoulders relaxing. "No, I think

it has something to do with the Unhallowed's end game."

"My four-hundred-year-old embarrassing moment has something to do with their resurrection plot? Do tell."

"Damned if I know, but the spirits never come out and say exactly what they mean. I think they want to, but they can't, so they're limited to visions and riddles."

"More like they won't," Nye muttered. "There's another mystery for you, Gabby. Who controls the spirits?"

"That's deep," she retorted.

"So what was it about that day..." he mused, thinking over the proceedings. The way he was lead into the forest like a lamb to the slaughter, the rune Eleanor was carving into his forehead, the spell she was in the midst of casting when he sliced off her head... Or was it something unseen?

"If I can attempt to scry the rune on your chest, maybe I can find a clue," she was saying. "I could only see through Eleanor's eyes. I wasn't privy to her thoughts. And the rune she was carving back then was incomplete."

"But it's gone," he said, snapping to attention. "It healed days ago."

"Traces might still linger. It's worth a shot either way."

"So I gather that means your battery is charged now?"

She shrugged.

He scowled in return, rubbing at the tingling sensation that had risen in his flesh at the mention of the rune.

"Do you mind?" Gabby asked, gesturing to him.

"Do you want me to do a striptease for you?" he asked with a smirk.

"Don't be a smartass. I want to check you for any residual magic. If I can get a sense for Eleanor's rune, I might be able to decipher the intent."

"We already know her intent," he all but spat. "I felt the power flowing through me. I heard the voices."

"You heard the voices?" Gabby parroted, straightening up in interest. "You mean, you heard the spirits?"

"What spirits?" he asked sullenly.

"The ley lines are a direct conduit to the earth's energy," she explained. "I can access them through the spirit realm, though I can't tap into their energy. I can only watch and listen. When I communed with them that night, I was guided by the ancestor spirits." She shook her head in bewilderment. "They spoke to you?"

He ignored her question and asked, "Whose ancestors?"

"*Everyone's,*" she said pointedly. "Though only the witches speak to me because we have a common interest in the living. What did you hear?"

"What does it matter?"

"It could matter a great deal."

Nye scowled and stared off into space, mulling over the night of the ritual. The moment the power of the ley lines had flowed through him, his mind had been filled with nothing short of chaos. His body wasn't designed to hold any kind of magic other than what already kept him alive, so through the pain, he hadn't heard much of anything other than an unrelenting hum of drowned voices. Until then, he'd thought it was a product of his own insanity.

"I can't remember anything," he muttered.

Gabby sighed in mild annoyance. "Okay, but at least let me examine your chest."

Knowing he wouldn't escape her constant questioning, he stood and unbuttoned his shirt. Lying on the floor, the witch knelt beside him and placed her palms over his sternum.

"So how were my skills?" he asked with a smirk. "I've had time to practice since then, but one never forgets the fundamentals."

"What are you talking about?" Gabby asked, cocking her head to the side.

He made a kissy face at her and laughed as her cheeks turned scarlet.

"Shut up," she hissed. "I need to concentrate."

Allowing her to settle, he didn't move as her fingers probed his chest, rising and falling with the hard ridges of his muscles. Her skin heated as her power flowed into him, the energy tickling his nerve endings as she scried his flesh for clues.

Abruptly, the study door burst open, and they both glanced up at the sudden intrusion. Isobel stood over them, a deep-set scowl on her face. Nye knew what he and Gabby must look like, but it couldn't be any further from the truth. Though if looks could kill, then the witch was a dead woman.

"Hello, darling." He smiled at Isobel, throwing in a wink for good measure.

"What are you doing?" she asked, her voice tight.

Gabby flushed and pulled her hands away from his chest. "It's not what it looks like," she said hastily. "I'm scrying."

"Scrying?" Isobel's gaze shifted from him to the witch and back again.

"Don't look at me," he said with a shrug. "I don't speak witch."

"I'm looking for any residual marks the rune may have left behind," Gabby explained. "Just to be sure."

"And?"

Nye raised an eyebrow, his expression asking the same question.

Gabby frowned and rubbed her eyes. "I'm not sure yet. I need to think about it."

"As long as I don't sprout a second head," Nye declared, sitting up. "This one is big enough."

Isobel stormed from the room, clearly upset over nothing at all, and he rose to his feet, following her out into the hall.

Grasping her hand, he tugged her back into his

arms. "Jealousy becomes you," he murmured, stroking her flushed cheeks. "I like it."

She moaned softly. "What have you done to me, Nye?"

"What have I done to you?" he asked in surprise. "Dear Isobel. What have you done to *me*?"

Chapter 4

Gabby watched as Nye followed Izzy out of the study.

Knowing exactly how tumultuous a relationship with a vampire could be, she cut her friend some slack. Never being able to feel as deeply as Nye would cause doubt to flourish where there needn't be any.

Sighing, she turned back to her grimoire and settled on the floor again. Picking up her pen, she flipped through the pages and worried over the absolute lack of information scrying Nye's chest had given her. The rune still lingered as she'd suspected, but it was faint, tendrils of power evaporating as soon as she touched it. Much like the curse markers she sensed in Isobel, the ritual had left its remnants in the spy.

Whatever rune Eleanor carved back then had everything to do with the one she'd placed on Nye for the ritual. Up until now, Gabby had believed the wraith was just using his ability to heal so they could siphon the ley lines at will. But what if was something else?

The day Nye took Eleanor's human life, he'd already been marked by the Unhallowed. What if all of this wasn't revenge? What if they were trapped into finishing what they'd started?

All of this was in aid of resurrecting the dead coven, and in order to achieve it, they needed whatever was locked inside the Keeping Place. Gabby couldn't make any sense out of it. Necromancy was dark magic and forbidden. It was a long-forgotten art, much like the existence of wraiths had been. If she understood it... No, that was a far too dangerous path to walk considering the dark power lingering in her veins. She'd been able to control it when she'd overwhelmed Eleanor and her wraiths, but that was a total fluke.

The map that had led them to the standing stones had called the stones the Keeping Place, but she'd learned that it wasn't there at all. Was the ritual to create some kind of key? Was Nye the missing link?

If Nye was the key and Eleanor was the bearer... Damn, how her head hurt!

"Gabby!"

She shot to her feet at the sound of Nye's panicked voice, her grimoire falling to the floor with a thud, and burst out of the study. Barreling into the hallway, her heart skipped a beat as she saw Nye bounding up the stairs. Isobel was cradled in his arms, her eyes drooping and her body slack.

"I'm fine," she muttered, her voice slurring slightly as they lingered on the landing. "I just stayed up too late last night."

"People don't collapse after a late night of talking," he scolded her. "You didn't even have anything to drink."

With a pang of dread, Gabby placed her palm on her friend's forehead, feeling for the curse markers, hoping her instinct was wrong.

Immediately, she felt the stirring of the black poison, and her expression fell. Her gaze met the vampire's and a look passed between them. They didn't have to say it. Isobel's curse was beginning to flare, which meant...

"I'm going to set you down in the study," Nye murmured to Isobel, his lips brushing against the top of her head while his gaze never left Gabby.

Carrying her back into the room, he gently placed her into his favourite armchair and turned to Gabby.

"Why now?" he asked, not bothering to keep his voice down. "Why so soon?"

"Her power must be growing again," Gabby muttered, sifting through her grimoire. She hadn't completed the spell, but she had no choice. She'd have to wing it.

"Great," Isobel said with a moan as she sank

further into the chair. "So I'm going to be wraith toast again? That's what this is, right?"

Gabby glanced at her friend but didn't confirm. How could she tell her friend that after all they'd done—after all Nye had sacrificed—it had all been for nothing.

Isobel seemed to get it without verbal confirmation and rolled her eyes. "Nice knowing you."

"Don't say that," Nye scolded her.

Gabby rubbed her eyes and declared, "Don't worry just yet. I have a plan."

"You do?" was Nye's reply. He didn't sound convinced. "Where was this plan the first time?"

"I didn't have enough time then," she exclaimed, her temper rising. "I thought I did now. We had no immediate leads on the wraiths, so I put my energy into finding a cure for the curse."

Nye raised his eyebrows. "But you said there was no cure... Anyway, Eleanor lifted the curse. It should be gone." His fist slammed down onto the surface of the desk with a bang. "*It should be gone!*"

"It's not," Isobel declared behind them. "It never went away."

Nye turned to face her, his expression softening. "But... How do you know?"

Isobel glanced at Gabby and shrugged. "You didn't have to tell me. I could feel it these past few days. I've been tired, and no amount of sleep was helping. I thought it was stress, so I stupidly ignored it. I should have said something."

Gabby nodded gravely, causing Nye's anger to rise further.

"You knew, didn't you?" he asked, seething. "All this time, you knew it could come back."

"Nye, leave her alone," Isobel said, her voice beginning to slur.

"I knew, but there was no point worrying you just yet. I'm surprised just as much as you are."

The spy flung his hands into the air. "Great! Just...*great*."

"I have a plan," Gabby went on. "I went to see a contact last night who gave me the means to help. I haven't had time to finish the spell, but I'm positive I know how to make it work."

"What contact?" Nye demanded. "A witch who knows how to cast a curse is no friend of ours, Gabby."

"I doubt a little old lady would dare cross me. Not after the conversation we had."

Gloria had been nothing but willing to help after she'd explained the ways of the world. Black, white, grey. There was no clear-cut good or evil. Not anymore. Besides, all she had to do was let slip to her good friend —Aya, the Witch Hunter—that there was a witch out there selling curses for a profit, and Gloria's power would be no more. The poor dear was well over the eighty-eight years she claimed and was hanging onto life by a thread. The moment her power was gone was the moment she ceased to be. She wouldn't even know what it was like to live without her earth magic. Long story short, Gabby trusted that Gloria had given her the goods.

"You're kidding, right?" Nye all but yelled. "You're putting Isobel's life in the hands of some little old lady's hearsay?"

"A little old earth witch with a very specific talent, I might add. Besides, we knew Eleanor would come back," she snapped, shoving him out of the way. "It was never a matter of if. Only when."

"Nye..."

They glanced at Isobel, who had managed to push herself up and out of the armchair. She laid her hand on Nye's shoulder, leaning against him for support. Gabby could see the exhaustion in her friend's eyes growing, and it was alarming how quickly the change was coming on. She didn't know what it meant, but it wasn't anything good.

"If we don't let Gabby try, then it's only a matter of time," Izzy said, taking Nye's hand. "Either way, Eleanor is coming, and worrying about me is not going to help you face her."

He turned, cupping her face in his hands. "Isobel..."

"We knew this might happen," she reasoned with him. "I've known Gabby a long time. I trust her."

Gabby fidgeted, suddenly embarrassed to be witnessing such a tender moment between her friends.

Her heart ached with memories of Regulus and their short time together, and she turned to retrieve her grimoire from the floor. She'd had a similar moment with him when he was dying, taking his mind back to his childhood home in the Italian hills to ease his passing. Unlike now, there'd been no hope of saving the Roman from his fate.

Tears stung her eyes as she flipped through the pages and pages of spells and research she'd scribed and found the one she'd been working on to halt the spread of Eleanor's degenerative curse. In the state it was, it could barely be called a doodle, let alone a spell to save her friend. She'd have to feel her way through it.

"What do we need to do?" Nye asked over her shoulder, signalling Izzy had convinced the vampire to let her help.

"There isn't a cure, that much I found out for sure, but there's something that can possibly halt the effects. It's like a sunlight spell," she muttered.

Nye closed his eyes for a moment, attempting to rein in his temper. "Can't it be transformed into a web?"

Gabby shook her head. "Perhaps, but not yet. No one I know of has even created a talisman to halt a curse, let alone a web. Right now, I need something to spell. Something that can be worn."

"Jewellery then," Nye said. "What kind?"

"A ring, a necklace... Something with a gemstone. Any kind will do, but it has to be genuine."

Nye glanced at Isobel, who had leaned back against the desk while they argued about her welfare. Her skin had begun to dull, taking on a rather alarming shade of ash. The first time Eleanor had cast the curse on her, it had taken hold quickly, draining her to the point of utter exhaustion within twenty-four hours. No doubt, the same thing would happen again. If the spell weren't cast now, then Isobel would be bedridden by the end of the day.

"I don't have anything," Isobel said with a moan. "I never wear jewellery."

"I don't have anything on hand, but..." Gabby turned on her heel and began to rummage on bookshelves where there were various nooks and crannies filled with various crystals and herbs.

Many of the trinkets had been left behind by Regulus, treasures he'd collected from witches over the millennia and items he'd procured himself. Gemstones and crystals could be imbued with a variety of charms and wards, their energy reverberating in harmony with the earth. The ones she found hidden here were small, ranging from the size of a quarter to that of a nickel, and had long since lost their charge to time. None of them were set anyway.

"What about a jeweller?" came Isobel's voice. "Surely..."

"I said genuine," she replied, fossicking through

another shelf. "I won't trust the rocks from a random store on this. One little flaw twisted through the stone the wrong way could make things infinity more difficult than it has to be."

Izzy snorted. "Right now, I wish I was a geology major."

"I have something," Nye said suddenly.

The witch turned and stared at him. "You do?"

He nodded. "You're sure we have nothing else?"

"Nothing one hundred percent viable on a tight turnaround. What kind of gem is it?"

He narrowed his eyes. "Ruby."

"It'll do," Gabby said. "I'll begin preparing the spell while you get it."

"I don't even get to pick the necklace I'm going to wear for the rest of my life?" Isobel complained. "It had better not be ugly."

Nye flinched slightly, causing Gabby to pause. An uncomfortable Nye was something she'd never seen before. There was a story there, and by the way he'd reacted, a significant one, but there wasn't time to press him about it.

As he ghosted from the study, she cast all other thoughts from her mind and focused on the spell.

One mammoth task at a time.

In the opposite wing of the manor, Nye stood beside his bed and held a little wooden box in his palm. He'd hidden it among his things for a very long time, never once opening it and revealing its contents.

Isobel would kill him if she knew where it'd come from, but it was the only thing they had right now that Gabby could use as a talisman. The stone had to be genuine and pure...and he now held the purest ruby he'd ever seen in his hands.

The lid creaked as he opened it, and for the first time in two hundred years, the amulet within was revealed. The last time he'd laid eyes on it was when he'd placed it on the soft velvet and closed it away, never intending to look upon it again. Why he'd kept it all this time, he never knew.

Nye picked it up, the silver chain slipping through his fingers like silk. The pendant was heavy, the Celtic knot expertly handcrafted with immaculate intricacy, and the ruby gemstone, set within its strands of pure silver and gold, bright. Its facets sparkled as he turned it in the light, memories he'd carried with it penetrating his mind. A lot of shit had happened in his four hundred and whatever years of vampirism. A lot of shit.

Dropping the pendant back inside the little box, he snapped the lid closed. It was no coincidence that things were happening the way they were. The resurfacing of the curse, the spell that could halt it, the pendant being the only item in the whole manor that was suitable... The universe, or Gabby's ancestor spirits, was playing yet another trick on him.

Dammit. With Eleanor on the rapid rise to renewing her assault, he knew there was no avoiding it. They had learned nothing since the ritual and were floundering just as they had this entire time. The pendant had confirmed it, the sign blatant. He'd have to go see the Triskele.

When he returned to the study, Alex had appeared, and as per usual, he didn't look happy.

"Here," he said, handing Gabby the box and avoiding all eye contact with the founder. Alex remained silent, but he could feel the anger radiating off him in waves.

Taking his place beside Isobel, who had returned to the armchair, he placed his hand reassuringly on her shoulder. Whether he was attempting to comfort her in her hour of need or soothe his own pride, he didn't know.

Gabby opened the box and whistled. "This looks old."

"That's because it is," he replied.

Showing the contents of the box to Isobel, a pointed look passed between them, and Nye scowled. *Women.*

"Is it suitable?" he prodded.

"It's perfect," the witch replied, sitting cross-legged on the floor. Laying the pendant on the pages of her grimoire, she added, "The stone is completely flawless. How did you get it?"

"It was a long time ago," he said flippantly, aware that everyone was staring at him. "I can't remember."

Thankfully, the questions stopped as Gabby got to work. They watched on as she began to mutter under her breath, speaking the words of the spell. Even if they could hear her clearly, there was no way he'd be able to understand the language she spoke. Obviously, witch speak could only be deciphered by a witch. No translation had ever existed for the mere fact magic had never allowed one to be.

Nye felt Gabby's power charge the space around them as she progressed, her palm hovering over the pendant. For a moment, the air seemed to shimmer and flare before finally subsiding. Then she opened her eyes.

"It's done," the witch said, picking up the necklace and handing it to Isobel. "Give it a try."

Isobel raised her hands, circling the chain around her neck. She fumbled with the clasp, cursing when she couldn't get it to close, and Nye gently pried it from her fingers.

"Allow me," he murmured.

She swept her hair aside as he lowered the pendant around her neck, the chain settling against her ivory skin. Securing the clasp, he let it go, his fingers brushing against her neck. *It had to work...*

He watched closely as Isobel picked up the

pendant and turned it over in her fingers. When she was done examining it, she smiled up at him. Breathing a sigh of relief, Nye allowed his lips to curve into a returning smile.

"How do you feel?" Gabby asked, watching her friend.

Isobel shook her head and blinked a few times before saying, "Fine. I feel just fine. It's like..." She glanced up and shook her head. "It just went away."

The witch studied her for another moment and declared, "The curse has retreated, but the markers are still there. The pendant should hold it at bay as long as you keep wearing it. *Damn, Gloria.*"

"Don't worry about it," Isobel said wryly. "It'll never leave my neck. Luckily for me, it's pretty."

Nye knelt beside her and remained stoic. "Good," he said. "We can deal with that. It's manageable."

"Now what?" Alex asked. "Obviously Eleanor is powering up..."

Nye mulled over his past relationship with the Triskele and began to feel uneasy. They hadn't parted on the best of terms despite their allegiance. Would they welcome him back? Would they even remember? Thinking about their fearsome leader, he knew she had a long memory. It was a fifty-fifty chance he would be walking into a snake pit.

"I have some old...*friends* I can meet with," he said uneasily. "They have a past with the Unhallowed. They might be able to assist. There's bad blood there."

"Between you and them or the wraiths?" Alex asked with a sneer.

"The wraiths," he shot back. "You might want to think the opposite of me, but I made many favourable alliances while I was the leader of the Six. It was a long time ago I met with them, and not all have forgotten."

"Who are they?" Gabby asked warily, picking up on his apprehension.

"A werewolf pack."

"Werewolves?" Isobel exclaimed, sitting to shocked attention. "*Are you serious?*"

"You've seen witches, vampires, fae hybrids, Celestines, wraiths, and zombies," Nye declared, ticking each off on his fingers. "And you're surprised to hear about werewolves?"

She settled back into the armchair. "Point."

"They might not be entirely willing to help," he went on.

"Then I want to go with you," Isobel declared. "The curse isn't a problem now, and I can help. I know people. If they need reasoning with—"

"Izzy, no," Alex interrupted her. "If anyone is going with him, it'll be me."

"You need to sit on the bench for this one," Gabby said to the founder. "You're still volatile."

"I'll say," Nye said with a roll of his eyes.

"I'm tired of being a burden," Isobel argued. "It's my life, you know. I have a right to fight for it as much as anyone else does."

It was bad news, taking her into the Triskele's lair while she wore that pendant, but it was part of her now. She would live with Eleanor's poison for the rest of her life. Besides, she was right. She had every right to fight for her life. Why shouldn't she come? He knew the Triskele and what they were capable of, and if things went south—which was a remote possibility— he'd be there to protect her. Honestly, Nye knew he'd be in more trouble if he made her stay behind at the manor.

"Fine," he said. "You're with me."

Her eyes brightened. "Really?"

"It's not a field trip, Iz," Alex grumbled.

"You've got this?" Gabby asked Nye pointedly.

He nodded once, secure in his assessment of the situation. "I've got this."

Chapter 5

Gabby leaned against the wall of the garage, watching as Nye drove off with Isobel.

The roller door began to lower, but her gaze remained fixed on the space outside until it had closed completely. She didn't like the fact her very human friend was going on a road trip with her vampire boyfriend to see a pack of werewolves. Especially since it had only been a few hours since she'd collapsed.

"I don't like it," Alex said, lingering beside her.

"Nye won't let anything happen to her," she replied, crossing her arms over her chest. "You need to cut him some slack."

Alex grunted, then promptly disappeared, leaving her to wonder if those two would ever see eye to eye. It would be a miracle if they did. Both were very protective of Izzy. Thinking about the people who would die for her, she came up empty and shook her head. Her friends cared for her—of course, they did—but it was a far cry from the protection of true romantic love.

"Hey."

She glanced up at the ghostly arrival of Reed, her thoughts scattering.

"How's Isobel?" he asked.

Her brow creased. She didn't know Reed had been in the house when Izzy had relapsed. "How..."

"I was looking for Tristan," he explained. "I overheard."

Gabby sighed. Reed had been good to them, regardless of his allegiance to Nye and the Six. He'd driven her around London without so much as questioning her intentions, he'd fought zombies in the garden, and guarded the manor against wraith attacks. Paired with his duties to Nye and the London vampires, Reed was a good sort. He'd been so good, in fact, that she'd forgotten he was able to lurk in the manor. Still, his unwillingness to share his past had her wary of reciprocation.

"Isobel is fine," she replied. "She's gone away with Nye for a few days."

"He'll look after her," he said, smiling at her.

"I know." Straightening up, she dusted her jeans with her palms. Sometimes, she forgot he was a vampire he was so...human-like. "So did you find Tristan?"

"That's the thing," he replied, looking worried. "He's not anywhere."

She frowned at the tone of his voice and stepped around him, pushing into the manor. "That's stupid. He's got to be someplace."

"Trust me, Gabby. I looked." He followed her as she forged a path through the hallways and up the stairs into the far wing. "I went to the pub. I went to the heath. I walked the streets he favours. I checked all of his usual haunts and nothing. Nobody has seen him since... Well, since you guys fought the Unhallowed."

Dammit! She'd been so distracted by her work finding a cure for Isobel's curse she had all but forgotten the knight. The compulsion Eleanor had put on him had violated him so irrevocably, he'd sunk into a deep depression. Nobody had gone to see him since Gabby had removed all traces of the spell. No one other than Reed. It seemed she owed the vampire another debt of gratitude. Still, it didn't excuse the way she'd treated the knight. Tristan na Tri Tor was far from an afterthought.

"Tristan is..." She frowned again. "He's not himself lately."

"I've known the guy a while," Reed said from behind her. "But in the last few weeks, he seems to have changed. This whole Unhallowed thing... Is there something else going on? Something Nye isn't telling us?"

"Are you questioning your leader?" she asked,

turning on him. Gabby knew full well they hadn't let on how dire things had gotten with the wraiths, let alone they were gathering the power to come back. As far as Reed and the rest of London knew, the Unhallowed were toast.

"No, not at all," he said, staring her down. "If there's a problem, I want to be able to help fix it. Simple as that."

Narrowing her eyes, she regarded him, her thoughts ricocheting between how handsome he was and a desire to understand why he was so unfalteringly loyal to Nye...and in turn, her.

She was just lonely. Always on the outer, Gabby had never really been part of the things she'd been fighting for. She had no coven, a family who despised she was a witch, she constantly straddled allegiances, and then there was the fact she loved a Roman vampire—one of the first, created by the witch who had betrayed her kind. Gabby just didn't fit anywhere.

Despite all the despair she felt, she was the one who everyone turned to. The pillar who was meant to stand tall and strong, never faltering. How was she meant to do that when she was always set apart? Perhaps that was the very reason her friends looked to her for guidance...and maybe it was why she kept gravitating toward Reed. He was the only one who'd asked if *she* was okay.

"Fine," she said warily before turning back to her

path toward Tristan's room. "But you're going to have to give me answers sooner or later."

"I don't doubt it."

Opening the door to Tristan's abode, Gabby stepped inside. Immediately, she was overcome with the presence of the vampire, and her gaze moved around the space. She'd never really studied it before, let alone been inside without Tristan at her side.

The room was sparsely furnished, and no decoration marked the walls. Knowing the knight, she wasn't surprised at the neatness. His time as a Knights Templar had been one of his defining moments as a human, and his training and values had crossed over when he'd turned. He'd spent long years marching with armies across Europe and what was now the Middle East on the Crusades, and traveling efficiently and as light as possible was pretty much his motto.

His bed was perfectly made, showing no signs of being slept in. The floor was spotless. Even the bathroom was devoid of soap scum and water spots on the shower screen. Opening the wardrobe, his clothes still hung inside, a few stray coat hangers littered among his standard uniform of black and grey shirts and slacks.

Running her fingertips across the surface of a shelf, she allowed her earth sense to trickle forth and probe the room. All the while, Reed watched her intently from the doorway.

Coming to a standstill by the bedside table, she

picked up a small leather-bound book and flipped open the cover. It was a pocket-sized illuminated version of the Old Testament of the Bible. Handwritten, it must be...a thousand years old. It was worn, its edges frayed and pulling apart from the spine, the leaves of parchment torn and faded. She'd never seen it before, but for Tristan to have carried it for as long as he must've, it had to be special to him. Why leave it behind? Unless...

He'd lost hope.

Gabby didn't have to search through his meagre belongings to know he was gone. His intent had left an uneasy feeling in the air, her earth sense tingling with it. He blamed himself for attempting to take her life. He blamed himself for being susceptible to Eleanor's compulsion. He believed he was weak. *Oh, Tristan.*

"He's gone," she muttered, placing the Bible back where she found it.

"Gone?" Reed asked. "Gone where?"

She shrugged. "I have no idea."

"Should I begin a search?" the vampire went on. "I can rally the Six and attempt to find his trail. Nye will want to know."

"No," Gabby said, her heart feeling heavy with regret. "That won't be necessary."

Tristan was gone, and he wasn't coming back. Not in her lifetime.

That night, Gabby couldn't stop thinking about everything that had happened in the last few weeks.

Eleanor had resurfaced a lot sooner than she'd anticipated. At the earliest, she'd thought at least a few months would pass before the wraith regained her power, not a fortnight! The other members of the coven—the wraiths who'd been present at the ritual—must've sacrificed themselves so Eleanor could survive.

There were good and bad things about that. The good thing was there was only one wraith to worry about. The bad? Well, the bad was that it was Eleanor. The biggest bitch in the entire world that had a grudge against Nye and everyone he held dear.

After finding out Tristan had left, Gabby had forced Reed to take her back to see Gloria. If anyone knew about the bad business of being a dark witch and profiting from it, then it was she.

As per their previous arrangement, Reed made himself scarce the moment he dropped Gabby off outside the earth witch's apartment. He would wait in the wings, and when she was ready to depart, he would appear.

Standing on the stoop, Gabby cast one last look around the dark street, watching closely as a few cars *swished* past, then turned and knocked.

The door opened a moment later, revealing Gloria, and when she saw Gabby, she scowled. She wasn't pleased with the repeat appearance, especially since it was announced. Bad things followed Gabby, and the witch obviously didn't like any uninvited trouble worrying her at her age. Considering the people she welcomed into her floral wallpapered living room, the notion was almost comical.

"Oh, it's you." Her gaze took in the young witch with an air of annoyance, her gnarled fingers tightening around the edge of the door.

"Yes, it's *me*." Gabby had expected the attitude, especially since she had to strong-arm the little old lady into giving her the spell to save Isobel from the curse. It wasn't on the list of her proudest achievements, but knowing the sweet lady in the fluffy pink slippers was selling legitimate curses for a few thousand pounds a pop, she let her conscience off the hook.

"Did what I give you work?" Gloria asked.

"Yes."

"Then we're done here."

As Gloria went to shut the door in her face, Gabby allowed her magic to burst forth. The door swung inward, torn from the little old lady's grasp, and banged against the wall.

"No, we're not," she declared, narrowing her eyes in annoyance.

Gloria didn't look too pleased. "You put a hole in the plaster!" she exclaimed with a *humph*. "I hope you're going to fix that."

"Are you going to invite me in?"

"You don't need an invitation, dear," she said

turning her back and shuffling her way into her apartment. "You'll just push in, anyway."

Closing the door behind her, Gabby said, "It's important, Gloria. You're the only one who might be able to help."

"In trouble, are you?" she asked with a roll of her eyes as she sank down into her floral armchair.

"You know about unscrupulous things," Gabby began, taking a seat on the matching settee.

"Obviously, considering the topic of our last conversation."

There was no use hedging around the question. "What do you know about wraiths?"

"Wraiths?" she exclaimed, her eyes practically widening to the size of saucers. "Nothing at all. You had best leave."

Gabby didn't like the idea of bullying a little old lady, no matter how crooked she was, but there wasn't any other option. Gloria didn't want to help, either that or she was afraid of what would happen if she did. The only way she was getting answers was if she made some very specific threats.

"You know, Gloria," she began. "I have a friend with a very peculiar talent. An expert tracker with a blue fire that steals a witch's light. I'm sure you've heard of her."

"The Witch Hunter?" Her mouth fell open, and she began to panic. "You wouldn't!"

"Then help me," she said. "Gloria, you know

something. I can see it written all over your face. I don't need to be a witch to tell you're afraid. We need to stop them before it's too late."

"No, no, no," the witch said, pouring herself a cup of tea. Her hands shook so much, the pot almost ended up on the floor. "Wraiths love hallowed ground. They don't care about the hallowed part. Nothing keeps them out."

Gabby shivered, her gaze turning toward the window and the church that sat next door. St. Augustine's. A ley line must run underneath it, which meant...

"Gloria, this is important," she said firmly. Taking the witch's hand, she poured her good intent into her flesh, hoping her power would soothe the elderly lady. "Those wraiths... Right now, they're scratching away at survival, completely powerless until they leech off a ley line. They want to be resurrected. They want their human bodies back. I think you understand what will happen if they achieve their goal. *No one will be safe.*"

Gloria's gaze fixed on hers, and her grasp tightened. Power began to hum from the old witch, and Gabby smiled.

"I was at the farmer's market," she began, her voice wavering. "The jam was plum this month." She swallowed, pulling Gabby closer. "I felt this God-awful chill pass by. That's when I saw her. She was walking among the parishioners, large as life itself. She had this look of satisfaction on her face like she'd eaten the most spectacular meal and her belly was full. Then she stilled, her smile fading…"

"What happened then?" Gabby prodded gently.

"She turned and looked straight at me. Her eyes were like storm clouds…and it was if she knew what I was and what I'd been doing."

"What did she look like?" Gabby already knew who the woman was, but she needed Gloria to say it. She needed the earth witch to make her fear a reality.

"She was young, a wisp of a thing, her hair was the colour of chestnut, and it flowed around her in a mess of wild curls…"

"*Eleanor.*"

"I've known evil, dear, and she was more than that. I knew what she was without having ever seen it before. She was a wraith."

"Did she try to hurt you?" Gabby asked. "Did she speak?"

Gloria shook her head. "I left immediately and came home."

"I'm trying to stop them," she said. "Anything you know about wraiths or that woman, I need you to tell me. They want something that's being held in a place they call the Keeping Place."

Gloria narrowed her eyes and pushed out of her armchair. Shuffling into the kitchen, she busied herself in the cupboards, taking out a teapot and some cups and saucers. Opening the refrigerator, she picked up a pint of milk and hesitated.

"You're looking for a place. A building or a point on the earth," she finally said, arranging all the items on the kitchen table. "There are many other places something can be kept."

"Then what else could it be?" Rising to her feet, Gabby went to assist her. Picking up the electric kettle, she turned on the tap and began to fill it.

"I think it's—"

Behind her, the china rattled, and a cup fell to the floor, shattering on the parquetry. Dropping the kettle into the sink, Gabby turned and found the elderly witch leaning against the table, her entire body quivering.

"Gloria?" she asked, laying a hand on her shoulder. "Are you all right?"

She turned, her pink slippers shuffling on the floor, and when her gaze met Gabby's, it was full of raging storm clouds. Gabby gasped in horror as the little old lady's forehead flared, a rune burning into life. She hadn't escaped Eleanor at all!

"Gloria?" She grasped Gloria's hand and readied her power. "Gloria? Can you hear me?"

The witch moaned softly, then her head snapped to the side, her neck breaking in one swift motion.

"Gloria!" Gabby exclaimed, rushing forward to catch Gloria's frail body in her arms.

Gently lowering her to the floor, a curse slipped from Gabby's lips. There was nothing she could do. Gloria was gone.

Closing the witch's eyes, she knelt over her body and whispered a prayer in the witch language. Eleanor had used the poor woman as a spy in her twisted game. Gloria wasn't an innocent, not by a long shot, but no one deserved to be used as a puppet. No one.

Gabby racked her brain, trying to think of what she'd said to Gloria. If she'd let something slip about their plans, it would be bad. *Very bad.*

Knowing Eleanor was on the prowl and that it would only be a matter of time before she came her looking, Gabby pushed to her feet. There was nothing she could do for Gloria's memory. Not right now. No, at this moment, she was more worried about Reed, who was outside waiting for her while a crazed wraith was stalking the streets. She wasn't ready to face Eleanor, not yet. She'd have to grab the vampire and run.

Striding from the apartment, she lingered on the street, looking frantically for Reed.

As if on cue, the sleek black sedan came rolling down the street and stopped before her. When she didn't move from the stoop, Reed got out of the driver's side and rounded the car.

"What's—"

He didn't have a chance to finish asking his question. She forced him up against the side of the car, holding him in place with all the power she could muster. Grasping his face, she peered into his eyes, searching for any sign that he'd wrangled with a wraith while he'd been out here waiting for her.

His chest heaved against hers, his confusion clear, but he didn't try to fight her. He sank into her touch with a willingness that excited yet terrified her. Either he was an extremely good judge of character or he trusted way too easily.

Forcing her earth sense into his body, she pulled apart every inch of his consciousness she could grasp, sifting through each layer but came up empty-handed. Eleanor hadn't gotten to him.

Letting him go, she stepped away, her power retreating.

He stared at her with a quizzical look. "What was that about?"

"We need to get out of here," she replied, her body tingling from the memory of his pressing against hers. "Eleanor is lurking around here someplace. My contact was compromised."

"Bloody hell," he cursed. "Get in."

Sliding into the back as he took the front, she cast one last look at Gloria's apartment and frowned. Who else needed to die before this was over?

She did know one thing. Whatever Gloria was about to tell her was important. They must be getting closer to figuring out the Unhallowed's plan. The problem was, Gabby still didn't understand what it was.

Chapter 6

I sobel reclined in the passenger seat of Nye's car, fiddling with the pendant he'd given her.

It was a pretty silver and gold Celtic knot with a stunning ruby in the centre, but she wondered why he had it. Had it belonged to someone in his family?

Ever since they'd left the manor in Hampstead, he'd been tight-lipped, his gaze fixed firmly on the road ahead of them. Outside her window, rolling green countryside flashed past as they powered down the motorway, traveling farther and farther away from the sprawling urban landscape of London.

Studying the facets cut into the ruby, she sighed softly. She had better get used to wearing it if she wanted to keep the curse from eating her insides out. What a way to die. Just falling asleep and never waking up...

"You okay?"

She glanced up at the sound of Nye's voice and smile thinly. "I'm okay."

He peered at the pendant for a moment before returning his attention to the road ahead.

"So who are these wolves?" she asked, dropping the pendant back down her blouse out of sight. "What do they have to do with the Unhallowed?"

"The Triskele," he replied. "They have a long legacy in this country. Their pack can be traced back well over fifteen hundred years."

"That long? Wow."

"They have a great deal of traditions," he muttered.

"So...is the whole werewolf myth true? The moon, the strength..."

"Pretty much," he replied.

She snorted and glanced out of the window. "So they might know something about the Unhallowed?"

"Their alpha used to be acquainted with Eleanor," he replied.

Her head spun back so fast she almost gave herself whiplash. "*What?*"

"I knew her long before I cut off her head," he replied stonily. "Eleanor ran in some unusual circles for reasons I never quite understood. It was a different time, and it was much easier to hide what we were... and what we were doing."

"Aren't witches meant to hate werewolves?"

"Not really," he replied, glancing at her. "It's just vampires who get the bad rap."

"So she was friends with an alpha wolf from the Triskele," she mused. "So the ancestors of this wolf might know about the Unhallowed through their traditions and stories?"

Nye smiled to himself and shook his head. "No, nothing like that. We're going to see the same alpha."

Isobel frowned, not understanding. "But werewolves are only meant to have a human lifespan. How..."

"Because the Triskele's alpha is more than just an ordinary wolf."

"It's the *same* alpha? How does that even work?" Isobel wasn't sure why she was surprised considering the things that kept happening around her. It seemed absolutely anything was possible.

"Like I said, there's history with Eleanor and the Unhallowed." He gestured toward the right-hand side of the car. "We're here."

Isobel didn't have time to ponder the situation further because the moment Nye turned the car off the road onto a private driveway, her gaze flew forward with interest. She never knew werewolves existed until few hours ago, let alone knew how they lived.

When a real life bona fide castle came into view through the trees, Isobel's mouth fell open. The bluestone structure was crumbled in places along the parapet, but it was otherwise intact. As they emerged through the forest and onto the grounds, she could see the medieval building had been built upon over the centuries, and now it looked like a large compound. Other buildings had been added to the original walls, and further afield, whitewashed cottages with thatched roofs pinpricked the clearing. If it weren't for the modern fixtures lingering here and there, Isobel would've thought they'd stepped back in time.

"They're quite fixed in their ways," Nye said dryly as he brought the car to a standstill. "And quite closed off to the modern world. They keep to their own, Isobel."

"Is that code for 'don't leave my side' because I wasn't planning on it." She stared through the windshield and up at the castle, wondering how many rooms there were inside. "I learned my lesson back in Oxford when that creep Aed kidnapped me, thank you very much."

"Best not mention that, either," he said. "Or about our current situation…and especially not your curse."

"So it's best not to open my mouth at all?" she snapped, irritated he thought she was that stupid.

"I didn't say that."

"If you were going to order me around like an imbecile, why did you allow me to come?"

Nye moved faster than she could follow, grasping her face in his hands. "I don't think you're an imbecile," he said, lowering his lips toward hers. "Far from it, actually."

"Then why do I feel like a moron right now?" she muttered, captured in his gaze.

"You shouldn't," he replied before leaning closer.

His lips met hers, and finally, he kissed her. A blaze of heat erupted through her body at his touch, and she curled her hands around the lapels of his suit jacket and tugged him closer. Entirely forgetting where they were, she almost threw herself into his lap.

A sharp knock on the window broke them apart, and Isobel started at the sight of a heavily built man standing outside the car.

"State your business," he growled, his eyebrow raised.

Rolling down the window, Nye said, "We're here to see your alpha."

He stooped down so he could peer across at Isobel, then nodded. "Come with me."

Sliding from the car, she met Nye at the front, his hand finding hers. Together, they followed the beast of a man across the threshold and into the castle. All around them, Isobel could smell the scent of wood smoke, earth, and the dampness a structure made completely with stone permeated. Here and there, tapestries depicting great battles of the past adorned the walls, and rugs in various stages of wear and tear coated the floor.

The man left them at the door of what appeared to be the main hall of the original castle, and she followed Nye inside, not wanting to be left behind with that creature. He was positively terrifying.

Immediately, her gaze fell on a woman who was

sitting alone beside the open fireplace. Her presence was overwhelming, and Isobel didn't have to be a genius to know she was someone who had a very supernatural way about her.

"Nye Saer," she purred, rising to her feet at their entrance. "You're a sight for sore eyes."

"After two hundred years, that's the welcome you give me?" he drawled, putting Isobel on edge. She knew he'd had a life before her, but she knew so little it made her uneasy.

The werewolf's attention turned to her, and she glanced at Nye.

"I am Sheera," the wolf declared, jutting her chin upward. "I am the Triskele alpha. And who are you?"

She was the alpha?

"I'm Isobel," she replied, her voice betraying her rising annoyance at the vampire who stood next to her.

The alpha looked like a Viking with her strong shoulders and athletic build. Her waist-length blonde hair had been twisted and plaited, braids holding the strands away from her face, which was also striking. Blue eyes stared at her with interest, her freckled nose twitching as her gaze lowered to Isobel's neck and back up. *Great...did werewolves like human blood, too?*

"You seem surprised," the alpha said to her. "I wasn't who you were expecting?"

"No, not at all... I..." She faltered, her resolve bending under the wolf's scrutiny.

"Who said an alpha couldn't be a woman?" Sheera declared.

"It's very twenty-first century," she offered.

Sheera stared at her for a moment, and Isobel began to fidget, thinking she'd stuck her foot in it completely this time, but the alpha began to laugh, her eyes crinkling at the corners.

"Some might say I was well ahead of my time," she went on. "Those born into the pack who swear allegiance to me will never be held accountable to the moon. We are a free people. I sacrificed my mortality so they could live without chains. A man would never do such a thing."

"Oh, don't try to sugarcoat it," Nye said with a snort. "You bind these poor sods to you so they can escape their transformation, but you never disclosed the fine print. Not in the time I knew you."

"Careful, Nye. There might be history between us, but I won't let it stop me from tearing off your head."

"She's their sire," he said to Isobel, completely ignoring the alpha's threat. "She tells them what to do, and they have no choice but to obey. Trained puppies."

"Is that natural?" was her reply, and Nye shook his head. It was most definitely not.

"If you've come here looking for favours, then you're not winning me over, Nye Saer," the alpha spat.

Rising to her feet, she prowled toward them, her eyes trained on Isobel. Standing before her, Sheera picked up the pendant that hung around her neck, hidden under her blouse. She stared at it for a moment, then narrowed her eyes before returning her gaze to Isobel's with renewed interest.

Isobel glanced at the wolf, then at the pendant. Triskele... Nye had given her a Triskele pendant. A pendant she had to wear at all times to stop her from wasting away. A pendant that she got the feeling had belonged to the woman standing before her. An *immortal* werewolf, no less.

Asshole!

"Sheera," Nye began, but Sheera held up her hand to silence him.

Isobel began to feel a chill spread through her bones and edged backward. The movement loosened the pendant from Sheera's grasp, and it fell back into place.

"I won't hear any talk from you today, vampire," the alpha said, her gaze still locked on Isobel's. "Business can wait. Tonight, you are my guests." She snapped her fingers, her attention moving to that of a young man who appeared at her beckoning. "Hastings, take these two to our best guest room in the castle. Then let Uma in the kitchen know there'll be a feast tonight. Then spread the word."

"A feast?" he asked with interest. "Right away."

Sheera turned to Nye and Isobel and gestured for them to follow Hastings. "I expect to see you both tonight. It may not be to your particular tastes," she said, her lip curling at Nye, "but your human will no doubt be thankful for a proper meal."

Nye practically glowered at the wolf and nodded. "Tomorrow, then. It has been a long day."

"Good," Sheera declared with a wide smile. "It was nice meeting you, Isobel. I'm sure we'll have plenty of time to get to know one another."

As Nye guided her from the room, his expression troubled, Isobel glanced over her shoulder at the alpha wolf as she watched them leave. There was smugness in her features that she didn't like at all, and her stomach quivered.

Something wasn't right about this, she was certain of it.

***

Nye walked hand in hand with Isobel through the castle, his nerves on edge.

He hadn't liked the idea of her accompanying him on this expedition, but she'd argued a very valid point. She was more than capable of helping in their quest, but the longer they dwelled in the Triskele's lair, the more he began to feel uneasy about it.

He knew he was going to stir some controversy with Sheera after turning up out of the blue, especially considering their convoluted past. The pendant was another ingredient in the pot, and he hoped Isobel would keep it hidden. He'd have to explain its significance sooner rather than later, but there was no time for it now.

They emerged into the hall where they'd been received that afternoon and found it much changed. It had been converted into a grand dining room fit for a pack of wolves. Two long tables ran the length of the room, and one smaller one sat at the head, no doubt for Sheera and her inner circle. Every surface was laden with bottles of wine and beer, and plates of various meats were being laid out as the pack began to fill the room, eager to settle down for a riotous meal.

As the noise level began to rise, Isobel's hand tightened around his, her gaze darting nervously around the increasing number of werewolves.

"So the Triskele are a large pack?" she asked. "Sheera saves all these people from turning during a full moon?"

Nye sniffed the air. "Most of them, yes."

Her eyebrows rose. "Did you just sniff them?"

"Believe me, they smell terrible. You don't want to experience it."

"Ah, there they are!"

Nye turned at the sound of Sheera's voice and dropped Isobel's hand. She'd changed from her casual clothing into more formal attire—if leather pants, heeled boots, a corset, and a light wrap over her shoulders was considered 'formal.' She looked like she would fit in more at an establishment of the night than a werewolf pack dinner.

Isobel tensed at the sight of the alpha, but she didn't drop her gaze. *Hold true, Isobel*, he thought to himself.

"Nye, you must accompany me at the head table," Sheera said with a smile. "Isobel, *darling*, I've asked some of my most loyal girls to entertain you this evening. They're great fun and a sight more interesting than boring talk between clan leaders."

Nye narrowed his eyes, knowing exactly what Sheera was playing at. She wanted to separate them and not because she was going to divulge a deep, dark secret.

"Oh," Isobel squeaked as three young women appeared and circled her. They began chattering happily among themselves, pawing at her fiery red hair.

"You'll be well looked after," Sheera said with an obviously fake smile. "The girls are a great deal of fun. *Aren't you?*"

The youngest woman threaded her arm through Isobel's and began guiding her away. Isobel cast a panicked look over her shoulder, and Nye nodded, signalling she should go. She'd be perfectly fine as long as he didn't lose his temper. If he stepped out of line and caused a scene, Isobel would be the first to go.

He didn't like that they'd been separated, but there wasn't much he could do to complain about it if they wanted Sheera to spill her secrets about her time with Eleanor. The alpha might hold the one piece of information that could save them all, and that was worth playing her game...for now.

"Isn't this much better?" Sheera asked as they took their seats at the head table. "Now we can talk freely, you and I."

"We can talk freely with Isobel," he spat, his fighters tightening around the stem of his wineglass. "There is no other talk we need to attend to other than what I came for."

"Isn't the human your pet?" Sheera cast a pointed glance toward Isobel. "She's a pretty thing, very much your type, I suppose. But isn't she a little too fragile?"

"No," Nye replied, glancing toward the opposite end of the table where Isobel sat, a look of anger etched on her face. "She is not a pet." Picking up his glass, he took a long draught of the earthy liquid to help calm his burning throat.

Sheera pouted. "Then why did you bring her into my home? Wearing that pendant, no less."

"She is as much a part of this as I," he said, ignoring her quip. "That is my fault, and she has as much right to seek revenge on the Unhallowed as any of us." He set down his glass and raised an eyebrow at her. "Why didn't you tell her the truth about your immortality? You know I'll only reveal it to her the moment we're alone."

"Which brings me to my next question. Why didn't you tell her the truth about us?" When he hesitated,

Sheera smirked. "See, Nye. We both have things that are best left to secrecy."

"Four hundred years of living takes a long time to divulge," he retorted. "If it's not important, *I forget it.*"

She laughed loudly, throwing her head back for added benefit. Across the room, he caught Isobel's eye. She looked positively sick to the stomach.

"I'm here for information on the Unhallowed. Nothing more." He turned to face Sheera, his gaze burning into hers. "There's no way you would have missed Eleanor's return."

He snatched her right hand and shoved up the sleeve of her blouse, revealing the rune seared into her flesh. A circle slashed with an inverted triangle crossed with three diagonal lines. The mark of an Unhallowed spell.

Sheera's lip curled in annoyance, and she pulled her arm away. Leaning in, her gaze dropped to his lips, and her tongue darted out to lick her own.

"The Unhallowed gifted me with immortality while they still held their humanity," she said, her finger tracing a path along the back of his hand. "I performed a task for them, and they rewarded me with my greatest desire."

"Power," he drawled.

"And you don't like a little of it yourself? Aren't you the leader of the London vampires in Regulus's stead?" She *tsk-tsked* and picked up her wine, pressing the glass against her lips.

"Believe me, it wasn't without a great deal of reluctance. I've seen what power does to people. Before and after I became a vampire."

"Oh, Nye, it all depends on what you do with it." She lifted her glass again, taking another sip. "What are you going to do with your power? I have a pack. You have an entire city."

"So what did she have you do?" he drawled, ignoring her question. It was blatant bait for a fight, and there was no way he was falling for it, not while Isobel sat across the room among fifty sire-bound werewolves. "It must've been a particular brand of fucked up if you got immortality and a get out of wolf-jail free card for your pack."

Sheera's lips curved into a sly smile. "Remember the time we were holed up in that cave off the coast of the Isle of Skye? The Unhallowed were tracking you if I recall correctly. You'd become separated from the Six, and there I was, ready and waiting to save the day." He tensed as he felt her foot wrap around his ankle. "The cave was a natural blind spot, and the rock reflected their magic, hiding us away until they'd retreated. The tide came in swiftly that day, brought by a torrential storm. How long were we trapped there by the waves? Two, maybe three days?" She traced a fingertip along his neck, applying pressure against his jugular. "I remember you were hungry...and not just for blood."

"That was a long time ago," he said thinly, brushing her hand away. "Things were different."

"I believe it was about two hundred years ago," she said with a laugh. "I can scarcely remember. Do you find that? After a few decades, the years just...run together, and all you can think about are the moments of passion."

"Like I said," he hissed. "Things are different now."

"I can see," she said, the smile never leaving her lips. "Tell me, Nye. Have you had her yet? The human, I mean. Have you showed her what *loving* a vampire feels like?" She leaned closer still, her lips pressing against his neck. She moved slowly, tracing a path across his jaw and to his lips. "I know exactly how it feels. In that cave, when you were joined with me—"

His hand shot up and grasped her face, pushing her away from him. She might be an immortal werewolf, but he was a vampire, and no matter how old she was, he'd always be stronger.

"Enough," he snapped. "I will not play your twisted games, Sheera."

She laughed softly, and her gaze flickered across the room. "Really? Then what have we been doing since the moment you sat down?"

Turning, he followed the alpha's gaze and found Isobel staring at them. Her expression said it all. Her beautiful face was twisted into a look of anguish as if he'd plunged his hand into her chest and ripped her heart clean from her body.

Nye tensed, readying himself to rise, but Sheera's hand slapped down onto his thigh, holding him in place. He watched helplessly as Isobel rose to her feet and strode from the room, her head held high.

"You're in trouble," Sheera cooed, her lips curving in triumph.

"What is this?" he asked, his temper rising. "Do you truly think I would bargain—"

"Darling," she interrupting him. "You'll sit and stay like a good boy. I'm not finished with you yet. We have a lot of catching up to do."

Nye ground his teeth together, swallowing his anger. There was nothing he wanted more than to follow Isobel and straighten things out, but if he did, he risked losing Sheera's good will, no matter how little of it he already had. Was this the cost of leading the London vampires? Was losing the only woman he'd truly loved the cost of protecting his city? Of protecting *her*?

Chapter 7

Isobel shut herself in the guest bedroom and resisted the urge to cry.

Ever since the ritual, Nye had hardly touched her, let alone kissed her. That moment in the car had been a rarity, and it stung. She wanted to feel the same passion he'd unleashed the night he'd bitten her, but it never came. All she'd experienced was a keen sense of frustration.

Sheera's hands had been all over him, and he'd done nothing to push her away. Not until she'd kissed him in front of everyone. Did he come here in hopes of finding something to help fight the Unhallowed? Or was he *exploring his options*? Isobel wouldn't be around forever, let alone look as young as she did now.

Picking up the pendant, she turned it over in her fingers, bile beginning to rise in the back of her throat. It had been Sheera's—she was certain of it. Why the hell would he let Gabby spell it, then bring her here, right to the scene of the crime? It didn't make sense.

Isobel couldn't help thinking they'd always been mismatched in some way. She'd followed her heart and declared her love for Nye, but was it ever going to be enough to keep them together?

Pushing off the door, she crossed the room and sifted through her bag, searching for her cell phone. Finding it right at the bottom, she unlocked the screen and scrolled through the contacts. Pressing Gabby's number, she held the phone to her ear and waited for her friend to pick up.

"Izzy, hey."

"Hey," she said with a sigh.

"Is Nye honouring his promise?" Gabby asked with a chuckle.

"He never mentioned these people to you?" she asked, keeping her voice low. "Not even once?"

"No. Why?"

"I'm pretty sure the alpha, who is a woman, by the way, is his ex."

"What?" Gabby exclaimed with a snort. "Nye and a werewolf? That's insane. Witches and vampires hate one another but vampires and wolves? That's an all-out brawl waiting to happen. Alliances, yes, but romance? No way."

"Gabby, you didn't see them together. She was all over him." Isobel bowed her head, clutching onto her phone for dear life.

"Don't tell me you feel threatened by her?"

"She's a glamazon *immortal* werewolf, Gabby. How am I supposed to compete with that? I'm going to get old and die, and she's going to look like a Victoria's Secret model for eternity. *Eternity.*"

She sank down onto the edge of the bed, her finger curling into the bedspread, which felt like a *real* animal pelt. She was all for acrylic when it came to cute, fluffy animals but werewolves? Isobel was beginning to wonder if skinning them for a quilt cover was the best idea out there. *A Sheera quilt.*

"I'm pretty sure the pendant was hers," she added, fighting back tears. "Why would he do that?"

"Have you asked him?"

She hesitated. "No, I haven't had the chance."

"I'm all for innocent until proven guilty," Gabby said gently. "Ask him. It mightn't be as bad as all that. Have the wolves told you anything about the wraiths?"

"No," she declared. "From the moment we arrived, she's done nothing but play games. She's told us nothing about the Unhallowed. Nothing at all."

"Keep working her, Iz. If she wants to play games, don't let yourself fall into her hands. Play back twice as hard. It's easier to fight inequality in the human world. There, we're only set apart by being women or by the colour of our skin. Here, we're set apart by our birthrights. You're human, so you're always going to have to be ten steps ahead of the curve. I wish it were easier, but that's the truth of it."

"Great," Isobel drawled. "Thanks for the constant reminder."

"Hey, I'm only trying to help. What else would you like me to say? Seduce Nye? That'll get his attention. Strip off for him. That'll soon fix his wandering eye."

"*Gabby!*" She was scandalised, but perhaps she was right. If she wanted to get to the bottom of their intimacy issues, then she'd have to push a little. But shove a vampire right into the situation that got her bit the last time? Tristan wasn't around to heal her this time, only a pack of mangy mutts. Speaking of the knight...

"Have you spoken to Tristan?" she asked. "Is he feeling any better? I feel bad for not seeking him out before we left. Nye was so flippant about it when I asked him."

"Listen, when you see Nye, could you tell him..."

"Tell him what?" She didn't like the tone her friend's voice had taken. It was if... Something had happened.

"Tristan's gone."

Her heart twisted. "Gone? As in...?"

"He left the night before your relapse," she replied. "I don't think he's coming back, Iz. Not in our lifetime."

"Shit." Isobel felt really bad for dumping her boyfriend problems on her friend when she was dealing with the loss of the knight. She didn't know how close they'd been, but he'd helped her out in more ways than she cared to acknowledge. Being imprisoned in the manor and only having him around to bring her food and answers had made her fond of the Irish vampire. To think he was gone...

"I'm sorry, Gabby," she murmured.

"No need to be sorry," was her reply. "It is what it is. He needed to go so he could make peace with what Eleanor did to him. We can't force him to stay." There was silence between them for a moment, before Gabby said, "Listen, are you going to be okay?"

"I'll be fine," Isobel muttered. "I'll deal just as I always have."

"It'll work out," Gabby said. "Nye loves you. Everything he's done...it's been to protect you. Never forget that."

"Right..." She sighed.

As the call disconnected, she stared at the screen as it turned blank, automatically locking itself. When there was a sound at the door, she straightened up, her heart leaping as Nye entered. Dropping her cell, she rose to her feet as he closed the door behind him.

"It was hers, wasn't it?" she demanded.

"What was?" He wasn't surprised at her outburst, which meant he was expecting her to give him a hard time.

"Don't play dumb, Nye," she snapped. "The pendant. Was it hers?"

"No," he replied with a growl. "It was not."

"I find it hard to believe when it's a bloody Triskele pendant!" she almost shrieked. "I'm not stupid! I saw the way she looked at it, and I saw her filthy paws all over you." She began to shake, tears threatening to burst forth in a torrential downpour. "*She kissed you.*"

"You can't be so foolish not to realise there were others before you, Isobel."

"A woman can hope," she snapped.

"It was unwelcome," he said darkly, closing the space between them. "If you didn't realise, Isobel, she separated us on purpose."

"I was..." She began to feel sick, the realisation of what had happened out there slowly sinking in.

"She would have had her little puppies tear you limb from limb if I didn't play into her hands." He stepped forward and grasped her shoulders. She attempted to twist away, but he was too strong for her. "After four hundred years, I was certain of the person I was. Who I was meant to be and then you knocked on my door..."

"You've hardly touched me since the ritual," she rasped. "You've hardly touched me at all."

"What do you want, Isobel?" he asked darkly. "I can do many things, but I can't read your mind."

She moaned softly, curling her fingers into his sweater. "Do you really need me to say it?"

His fingers speared into her hair, and he lowered his lips toward hers. "*It would help.*"

Her cheeks flamed red, and her heart sped up, galloping faster and faster as his body melded with hers, their embrace tightening. Knowing he could hear her pulse, she swallowed hard, the words stuck in her throat. It was easy to form the words in her mind, but saying them was another thing entirely.

"Shall I say it for you?" he asked, a grin pulling at his lips. "I never took you for demure, Isobel."

"Actions speak louder than words," she quipped.

Closing his mouth over hers, he kissed her hard, his tongue demanding entrance. She caved beneath his touch, allowing him to dominate, his movements awakening an insatiable need deep within her body. Her fingers hooked around the hem of his shirt, pulling the fabric from the waistband of his trousers.

Her body trembled under his expert ministrations as their clothing disappeared, his kisses becoming desperate and fast. His control seemed to be holding this time, his thirst for her blood at the back of his mind, but when he raised his head, she felt her heart skip as she beheld his eyes. Instead of a brilliant green, they were black as night. Not even an inch of white showed.

"You don't have to fear me," he whispered, pressing his lips against her neck. His breath fluttered along the curve of her shoulder, and she knew he was hiding himself from her lest she began to fear him. "I can't control my eyes, but everything else... I love you, Isobel."

He moaned softly as she coaxed his face back to hers. Looking into the darkness of his eyes, she traced her fingers over his cheekbones, lovingly caressing his scar.

"I'm not afraid," she replied, wrapping her arms around his neck. "I never have been."

He sighed, his lips parting, and he struck, kissing her with a strength she almost found overwhelming. He'd been holding back all this time...

Then after his final fear had been exposed, he lowered her onto the bed, giving her the exact thing she'd desired the moment his lips had first touched hers.

Him. Her. Euphoria.

Afterward, as they lay together, one word came to mind. *Epic.*

Gabby stared at the blank page in her grimoire and furrowed her brow.

The moment the rune flared on Gloria's forehead kept replaying over and over in her mind, and the sound of her brittle neck snapping echoed in her ears. She wasn't the most strait-laced witch, but she didn't deserve to die as a vessel of Eleanor's evil.

Still, what if Gloria was right? What if she was looking in all the wrong places? If the Keeping Place wasn't a point on earth, then where was it? In the spirit realm? Her visit had only given her more questions that had posed as answers.

Movement drew her attention, and she glanced up at Reed, who was lingering by the study door.

"I thought Eleanor was toast," he said. "What was she doing following you?"

She shook her head, feeling torn. He wasn't meant to know what she was doing, let alone come within inches of a wraith. A wraith who was meant to be dead as far as the Six and the London vampires were concerned.

"Tell me I can trust you, Reed," she said, glancing up at him. "I've gone along with Nye's judgment of you, but I don't know where we stand. You're evasive, yet you stand there with what looks like blind loyalty. I don't get it."

"What's there to get?" He shrugged. "I'm a soldier."

"You're also a vampire. I know nothing about you."

"I also know nothing about you outside of your reputation," he argued. "But does that stop me?"

Her eyes narrowed in warning.

"So Eleanor possessed that little old lady?" he asked, ignoring her.

"In a fashion," she replied, rubbing her eyes. "She was watching and listening. She never had control of her."

"But she had to be close? That's why you came to check on me."

"What? Did you think I was worried about your well-being?" she asked with a smirk.

"I think that's my cue to retire for the night." He

sighed and nodded his head. "Do you need anything before I go?"

"No, thank you."

She watched him leave, her mind swirling with too many conspiracy theories to worry about one vampire's intentions. Reed was a puzzle for another day.

Gabby couldn't even picture her future when she sat down and really thought about what she wanted. Not what her duty as a witch dictated but what she wanted in her heart. Love, companionship, a family. She'd fallen in love with a two-thousand-year-old vampire, a man she was supposed to hate, so how was that meant to go long term? Did she want to have children? She was the last of the Cohen line, so did that mean it was part of her duty to allow her heritage to continue?

The thought tumbled around her brain for a moment, and she sat up straight, her grimoire slipping from her fingers and falling to the floor with a thud.

The seed. The bearer of fruit. The Keeping Place... It couldn't be! It was the stupidest thing she'd ever heard, but it wasn't that farfetched. *Was it?*

To resurrect the Unhallowed, Eleanor would need considerable power. Power she couldn't get from the ley lines. She would need to create something that would be able to wield enough energy, and not just any object would do. Eleanor needed a witch. A living, breathing witch. Gabby was the most powerful alive, but even she didn't have the ability to bring back a whole coven from the other side.

Eleanor had to engineer a witch to be able to do it for her. A child that contained Nye's ability to heal and her witch legacy. But Eleanor couldn't carry a child, not as a wraith...

Dammit! The curse she placed on Isobel had to be half of the puzzle. The ritual they subjected Nye to was the other. All this time, they'd been looking in the wrong place.

As far as Gabby knew, Nye had been keeping his distance from Isobel since the ritual, and her annoyance with him had been rising. Despite him declaring his love for her friend, things hadn't got... physical. At least she didn't think so.

Snatching up her phone, she readied herself for the call she was about to make. How did she tell a vampire, who was meant to be infertile, not to have sex in case he unknowingly planted some kind of magical seed in her friend? *Awkward.*

There was no getting around it. She dialled Nye's number and hoped there was reception wherever he was. When the call connected and began to ring, she heaved a sigh of relief.

"This better be important," came his irritated voice.

"Nye, this is going to sound totally whacked, but don't sleep with Isobel."

"What the hell?" was his annoyed reply. "What kind of question is that?"

"You're the seed, and Eleanor was meant to bear the fruit. *Bear the fruit.*"

"What are you trying to say, Gabby?"

"She can't bear it anymore. Not after you killed her human body. She needed a new vessel."

"I don't understand."

Dammit. How could he be so thick? "I'm pretty sure the Keeping Place is..."

A second went by, and then he seemed to get it. "Isobel's uterus? *Bloody hell.*"

"Please, Nye. Until I figure out how to reverse whatever Eleanor's done..."

There was a long pause on the other end of the line, and then the words she was dreading came out of his mouth.

"Too late."

Chapter 8

S heera stared out over her empire and smiled.

She stood on the parapets of her castle, the light of the full moon bathing everything in a muted glow that seemed to turn the foulest of cesspools into shimmering silver oases.

Once, she would have been held prisoner by this night, her wolf side demanding to be brought forth. There'd been no way of stopping the transformation when she was a girl, and every month, all the bones in her body would snap and bend as her human body was shed. It was agony for all who were cursed to run with a pack. That was why Eleanor's bargain had tempted her so much.

In the distance, the lights of London were a blight on the horizon. This world was never dark, not like it was when she was young and mortal. The stars shone brilliantly back then, but now they had abandoned the earth.

Thinking about Nye, Sheera smirked. The fool.

"You're getting more predictable as the years go on."

Turning at the sound of Eleanor's voice, Sheera snarled. After hundreds of years and no word, she'd began to think the Unhallowed were dead and gone, their plans for resurrection dissolving along with them. Unfortunately, they'd only been biding their time as they gathered power for a full-frontal assault.

"Basking in the moonlight?" the wraith raised an eyebrow. "I would've thought you'd hate the moon, being what you are."

"You know very well that the Triskele are immune."

Her lips curved into a sly smile. "And who do you have to thank for that?"

"If you're here for an update, I don't have much of anything to tell you," Sheera stated. "You're jumping the gun as usual. A few hundred years of waiting, and now you're going to spoil it?"

Eleanor rested her elbows on the stone wall, her gaze fixing on the smear of light on the horizon. "You forget who holds all the cards here, wolf."

She said nothing, waiting for the wraith to say what she'd come here to say. In all the long years they'd known one another, Eleanor had always harboured a number of ulterior motives, and none of them were good. Much like the immortality she'd given her, it had come with a price…which she was still paying.

"Did it pain you to see them together?" Eleanor asked. "Walking hand in hand and gazing into one another's eyes?"

"I made the human jealous," Sheera snarled, "and Nye grovelled at her feet. What more do you want?"

"You still love him after all these years?" Eleanor asked with a snigger. "He never loved you. Not even while he had your body in that cave."

"I could have borne the child for you," she hissed. "I'm immortal. I'm strong."

The wraith laughed again. "You? A dog? I don't think so. Not after the curse I placed on you."

"And what about you, *wraith*?" she asked, turning Eleanor's spite back onto her. "You loved him once, too, if I remember correctly."

Her words didn't seem to have an effect on her. "Perhaps for a while, but I always knew it would never amount to anything. I took what I could while I was able. Then he became useful in another way."

"Your precious *seed*."

Eleanor remained silent, her gaze moving to the sky. Sheera waited, knowing she couldn't leave even if she tried. Remembering the day when her one-time friend had offered her immortality and immunity from the moon for her and her pack, her blood boiled. She'd been tricked, and it wasn't until it was too late that she realised the cost of saving her people from endless torment was too great. Nature should never be trifled with.

Sheera began to feel faint, her head swimming with fatigue, and she stumbled, her hands steadying herself against the stone wall. Her breath caught as she saw her skin begin to move. It trembled as if she was being shaken violently, and then it began to wither.

"What's happening to me?" she asked, her bones beginning to ache.

Eleanor smiled, her eyes glittering with malice. "Do you know what tonight is?"

Tonight? The full moon. Her gaze flew to the sky as she realised why the wraith beside her had appeared tonight.

"No, you wouldn't do this to them." Sheera gasped as she felt the life bleed from her body.

"Obviously, it's a full moon tonight, but not just any old moon. The humans call it a Super Moon. The largest to ever have graced the night sky in seventy years." She reached out her hand as if she could pluck the celestial body from the sky. "She's so close you can almost touch her…"

Sheera's leg snapped, and she crumpled to the ground with a cry of agony. Her entire body erupted with sweat, millions of tiny hairs sprouting from her skin, and her jaw cracked loudly as it began to elongate.

"I never understood why werewolves detested their change," the wraith mused. "I imagine it would be grand to travel the forests as a wolf. Humanity is such a stifling concept."

Sheera howled in pain as her spine shattered and fused, then her elbows bent backward, morphing into knees.

"How long has it been since you've changed? One hundred years? Two hundred? More?" Eleanor knelt before the alpha and smoothed back her hair. "Have you forgotten your true nature already? We must never forget where we came from, Sheera. *Never.*"

"Bitch," she managed to snarl before her tongue completely changed into that of a wolf's tongue.

"Perhaps," she replied. "But you gave up on the Triskele and their legacy the day you turned your back on your true nature. *The immortal wolf.*" Eleanore laughed softly as Sheera felt the last of her human form slip away. Rising to her feet, she bade the wolf to stand, and there was nothing Sheera could do to defy her. "More like *the immortal slave.*"

Sheera's wolf form stood as tall as Eleanor's breast, her fur as silver as the moon that hung in the sky. Her blue eyes shone in the firelight, her pink tongue licking her teeth as she stood waiting for the woman's command.

On the air, she heard the howl of a hundred Triskele wolves as their transformations were completed. The connection she felt between each member of her pack was strong, their sire bond linking her will to theirs. She shared in their fear, for many had just turned for the first time, and their exhilaration as each embraced their animalistic side. They were all connected this night. They would all hunt as one.

Eleanor's fingers scratched the top of Sheera's head, her thumb stroking the soft fur behind her ears.

"Now be a good dog, and bring me Isobel."

***

"Was that Gabby?" Isobel asked, stirring beside Nye.

Her entire body hummed in satisfaction, the deep sleep she'd falling into only solidifying the fact she wanted to spend every waking moment with the vampire who'd stolen her heart. She trusted him now, not that she hadn't before, but she knew something had changed.

His back was to her, his skin pale even in the warm light from the lamp. He set his cell phone down and rubbed his eyes.

"Nye, what is it?" she asked again, this time sitting up. Clutching the blanket to her naked chest, she placed a hand on his shoulder.

"I think we really stuffed up tonight," he said after a moment.

Her heart sank, and all the satisfaction she'd been feeling began to fade into dread. "What do you mean? Do you regret this?"

He turned, and the look on his face was so full of panic, she recoiled.

"This was Eleanor's game all along," he said. "You and I…"

"Me and you? Nye, I don't understand…" She began to tremble. It was over, wasn't it? He regretted being with her, a human. Had everything been a lie? "If you're going to break my heart, you could've at least told me when we got back to London. I'm still naked for heaven's sake!" She began to scramble from the bed, taking the blanket with her, all the while trying to fight back the barrage of tears that were threatening to overwhelm her. "I know I'm only a bloody human with durability issues, but I have a heart!"

"Isobel, I didn't mean…"

She ignored him as she scooped up her bra and began attempting to put it on under the blanket so he wouldn't be able to glimpse her flimsy mortal body.

"Isobel, stop." Nye appeared before her, his hands grasping her shoulders. "Listen to me."

"What?" She shook herself free. "You already said it, Nye. *We stuffed up.*"

"You're not listening to me," he said. "Bloody hell, you vex me."

She was over the emotional whiplash that was their relationship. "Then explain it!"

"Gabby believes she knows where the Keeping Place is," he said, attempting to soothe her. "She called to warn us."

"The Keeping Place?" Isobel parroted. "The thing

the Unhallowed are looking for? The thing that might resurrect them?"

The spy nodded. "She kept going on about the seed and the fruit..."

His gaze dropped to her stomach, and clarity began to flood her mind. Seed. Fruit. She studied this kind of thing, myths and legends and their impact on societies. She should have gotten it long before now.

"No," she said, shaking her head in disbelief. "You're saying..."

"The ritual..." Nye began, looking paler than he usually did.

"I'm pregnant?" she asked, her heart beginning to race. "*Pregnant.*"

Holy shit.

It wasn't possible. Vampires couldn't procreate. They couldn't. Nye said he couldn't have children.

She sucked in a few short, sharp breaths, attempting to stave off an all-consuming panic attack. She was having a baby? A baby. In nine months, she was going to squeeze a tiny person out of her...*there*. Was it even going to be a person? Would it be half-vampire? Would it have any humanity? Would it be born at all?

"You might be," he said. "Don't jump to conclusions just yet."

"Too late," she said. "I've already dived in head first. How is this possible? I mean, you're dead." She waved her hands at him, not even registering how naked they were standing there talking about a screwed-up miracle. "You're *dead*."

"Dead-ish," he said wryly. "Certain things aren't meant to work anymore."

"I don't get it…"

"The day she attacked me in the forest in the 1600s," he said as much to himself as to her. "She was trying to carve a rune into my forehead, but Regulus stopped her. I killed her then, taking out her human form. Whatever she started that day…"

"She's trying to finish."

"I'm sorry, Isobel," he pleaded, cupping her face. "I never meant for you to be dragged into this."

"I'm pretty sure you never expected her to come back."

"I never knew about her plans…"

"Nye, I believe you," she said, covering his hands with hers. "Eleanor is using me in her stead. I get it."

"I'm not sure you do," he whispered. "Gabby thinks the curse Eleanor put on you was to make you like her. To ready your body to bear the child."

Her breath hitched. "A wraith? I was going to turn into a wraith?"

"I don't know, but we need to leave. *Now*. After Sheera's games at dinner, I don't trust the Triskele. We shouldn't have come here."

"What do you mean?" Isobel asked as he turned and began to retrieve his clothes from the floor.

"Sheera was given her immortality by Eleanor. I

always knew this, but I never knew what she did for the Unhallowed in return. She and I always had an unsteady alliance. She helped me evade them once...”

“About two hundred years ago?” she asked with a raised eyebrow.

Nye hauled up his trousers and buttoned the fly. “About then.”

“What is it with you and your ex-girlfriends?”

“Listen, Isobel. There’s a great deal more to this story, and I will tell it to you, but now is not the time. We need to leave.”

Her pulse began to speed up, and she nodded. Picking up the rest of her clothes, she dressed haphazardly, mismatching the buttons on her blouse before shoving her feet into her boots.

Nye put his cell into his pocket as she stuffed the rest of their belongings into her handbag, thankful they’d traveled light. When they’d left the Hampstead manor, they hadn’t intended on staying overnight, not until Sheera had demanded they attend a feast after refusing point-blank to talk about the Unhallowed.

“She was stalling, wasn’t she?” Isobel asked, the pieces of the puzzle slotting together. “She knew about Eleanor’s plan... She tricked us into...” Her stomach heaved. “I feel sick.”

“Which is why we need to get out of here,” Nye said, grasping her hand.

If the ritual and the curse were cast for the sole purpose of a pregnancy, then one time was all it took.

There was an almost one hundred percent chance she was going to become a mother in nine months.

Tricked into having sex with her vampire boyfriend so she could get knocked up with a magical baby that was genetically engineered by a *wraith*. And she'd thought her kidnapping encounter with an insane vampire-fairy hybrid was whacked.

Eleanor needed the baby to resurrect the Unhallowed. That's what this was about, right? Isobel was nothing but an incubator, and as soon as the baby was born...end of the line.

"She's coming," she said, beginning to hyperventilate. "Eleanor's coming for me."

"Stay with me," Nye said, opening the bedroom door and peering out into the hall. "Remain quiet, and don't let go of my hand. I'll get you out of here, Isobel. Trust me."

"Alex is going to snap you in half," she babbled. "Knocking up his sister."

Nye turned and slid his hand over her mouth. "I need to you keep calm. Listen..."

She trembled under his grasp and did as he bade, the silence of the castle *whooshing* in her ears. Silence wasn't meant to sound like anything unless all those years of clubbing in her early university days had given her tinnitus. Then she heard it. A howl so full of pain, it lodged in her heart and twisted.

She tugged at Nye's hand. "Is that?"

"A wolf." He glanced at the roof. "Right above us."

As soon as he said it, a cacophony of answering calls sounded throughout the compound. Way too many for her to count.

"Nye," she began uneasily. "What happens when a wolf bites a vampire?"

"Nothing good," he replied, looking worried.

He tugged on her hand, and they began their flight through the castle, edging forward slowly in case they were met with resistance. The wolves would track them, hunting their prey with a heightened sense of smell and the intelligence of a human mind. She had to place all of her trust in Nye, but after the night they'd shared together, and after everything else...it was a no brainer. Isobel would follow him to the ends of the earth, no questions asked.

The sound of claws scraping on the stone floor echoed behind them as they twisted and turned through the maze of hallways and rooms in the castle. As soon as they found a route to an exit, Nye would pull her away, and a moment later, a wolf appeared. They were being herded.

Nye began searching behind tapestries as they went, looking for another way out, and it wasn't until Isobel was sure they weren't getting away that he found a concealed entrance.

Immediately, he pulled her into the darkened space, holding her steady as a wolf passed by their location. Glancing behind her, Isobel saw the spiral staircase, and her heart sank. The only way they could go was up. In the movies, everyone knew you weren't supposed to go upstairs, but the actors always did, and just when they thought they had gotten away from the serial killer, they popped out from underneath the bed and slashed the heroine to pieces. But this was real life, and it was either up there or back the way they came.

Nye made the decision for her, and once the wolf had passed the tapestry, they began to climb.

He led her higher and higher, her legs beginning to protest at all the stairs. It was a narrow space, likely the original staircase. Each step was twice as high as she was used to, her shoulders barely squeezing through the gap. Her right hand grasped the iron pole that ran directly up the centre, and her left held onto the rope, fixed to the wall with iron loops, for dear life.

Finally, they emerged out into the night, right at the top of one of the outer towers. There was nowhere to go but back the way they came or over the edge.

They were trapped.

A single lonely chair sat by the wall along with an empty coffee cup on the ground and an abandoned coat slung over the seat. A dark pile on the other side of the small tower turned out to be someone's discarded clothing. Whoever had been stationed here on watch had obviously changed into a wolf and had since scurried off to join the others.

Nye snatched the coat from the chair and sniffed it before placing it around Isobel's shoulders. "Here, this will mask your scent for now."

She clutched it tight, more in an attempt to shield herself from the pack than the cold. "What do we do now? We're trapped up here."

Looking over the edge of the tower, all she could see was the five-story drop to the ground below. When a group of wolves darted across the clearing, she stumbled back.

"Listen to me, Isobel," Nye said, forcing her to look at him. "You'll be safe here until I lead them away. Once you're clear, you need to run. Get a car, any car, and head back to the manor. I will meet you on the road."

"But how will you find me?" she asked, clutching him to her. "I can't leave you behind."

"Trust me," he murmured, his green eyes searching hers. "I will meet you on the road."

"But... What if I—"

"Don't," he said, interrupting her. "No what ifs. You have to."

He kissed her swiftly and then climbed up onto the parapet. He stood on the edge, balancing lithely, and glanced over his shoulder.

"Remember," he said. "I'll find you on the road." Their eyes met, and for a brief second, something profound passed between them, then he spread his arms wide and fell, dropping off the edge like an Olympic diver.

Rushing forward, Isobel glanced over the wall and gasped as she saw him twist through the air like a cat before colliding feet first on the ground.

Holy crap! That was her boyfriend?

The moment he hit, he sprang forth and disappeared faster than her human eyes could follow. A howl sounded on the air, then another, and soon, the pack began moving away from the castle. Whatever Nye was doing, it was working.

Turning toward the door, Isobel knew it was now or never. She had to make a break for it.

Chapter 9

Nye hit the ground and sprang forward, moving away from the tower.

He felt her lingering presence above as he heard the sound of the wolves as they emerged from the castle and the surrounding grounds. They were drawn by the sound of him hitting the earth, the thud echoing through the ground. With Isobel's scent masked, they would assume she was with him and give chase. All she needed was enough time to get out before Eleanor showed up.

The wolves would have been tasked with rounding them up and holding them until the wraith arrived. What would happen then Nye didn't want to know. If Isobel was pregnant...

Him? A father? The notion was as absurd as a vampire being able to procreate. Gabby was wrong.

There was no doubt in his mind that Sheera's sire

bond was in full effect, and it wouldn't be long before the entire pack knew his location. In their animal form, their minds would be linked and their senses in harmony to maximise the hunt. The hard part was not getting caught, but the harder part was not getting bit.

Darting through the trees, he sensed them following, the sound of their claws scraping on earth and their laboured breathing reaching his ears through the darkness. The light of the full moon filtered through the trees lighting his way even though he didn't need it. His vampire-enhanced eyesight was a match for the wolves that pursued him.

He banked left, sensing a presence breaking through the trees beside him. The shape of a large wolf emerged, its russet coloured fur streaked with sweat. Its jaws snapped as it caught his scent and weaved through the underbrush in an attempt to get closer.

Skidding to a halt, Nye clapped his hands, drawing its attention, and it did the same. Facing off with the vampire, it began to growl in warning, lowering its head and readying itself to strike.

"Here, puppy, puppy, puppy," Nye said, goading it into action. "You want me? Come here and *fetch*."

The wolf pounced, growling and snapping, and the spy dodged. Then he began running, leading the enemy from the castle and into the forest—far, far away from Isobel.

Hoping he'd given her enough time, he began to run faster in an attempt to lose the pack in the forest.

Then he would double back and meet Isobel on the road just as he'd promised. He couldn't fight a hundred wolves on his own, let alone Eleanor.

Breaking through a line of trees, he found himself in a clearing. On the opposite side, a dozen wolves emerged, leaping into the light of the moon.

Skidding to a stop, Nye's heart pounded wildly as he realised he was the one who'd been lured. Cursing, he turned, looking for a way out, but there was none. He'd been herded like a bloody sheep.

The wolves circled him, and every so often, one would dart forward and snap their jaws at his ankles before retreating back into line. More and more appeared through the trees, their eyes gleaming in the darkness. He was trapped in a sea of werewolves. The entire Triskele pack watched and waited, but none struck. They were waiting for their alpha.

Nye waited along with them, hoping Sheera was alone and not accompanied by Eleanor. His thoughts went to Isobel, and he hoped to all that was good in the world she'd had enough time to escape. If he didn't make it, then at least she would be able to get back to the manor. She'd be safe with Gabby and Tristan—if he was finished sulking—and Reed and the Six under the knight's command.

He didn't have to wait long. The wolves began to part, letting through their leader. The silver wolf was larger than the rest, but he didn't need to see her to understand who she was. He'd recognise her unearthly blue eyes anywhere, and they were still as prominent in her wolf form as her human.

"You don't have to do this," he said as Sheera stood before him, her head level with his chest. "You control the fate of your pack. *Your pack*, Sheera, not hers. Don't let Eleanor enslave your people."

Wolf-Sheera licked her lips before letting out a soft whine.

"I saved you once," he murmured. "Remember? When you were a girl?" She lowered her head slightly, listening. "Now it's time to save yourself...and your pack."

She began to growl softly, making her displeasure clear, but Nye wasn't finished. He had to convince her to take the noble path before they were all lost to the Unhallowed. He didn't care what happened to him, he couldn't allow Eleanor to resurrect her coven of wraiths...and he couldn't allow her to get her hands on Isobel.

"They'll be held to the whims of the moon, but isn't that better than being tied to a wraith?" he went on. "Think of what she'll ask them to do through you. Do you want that kind of suffering on your conscience?"

She lowered her snout, her eyes never leaving his. Was her movement a sign of her acquiescence?

"You sacrificed yourself once, and now you're the only one who has the power to save them from an eternity of slavery. You know what you have to do," he said, holding out his hand. "Break the sire bond, and set them free."

Wolf-Sheera padded forward and pressed her nose against his skin before rubbing her cheek against his palm. Unafraid, he knelt before her and stared into her shimmering blue eyes.

"I know," he said. "I won't leave you."

She butted her head against his chest and curled up on the ground, her chest beginning to heave as the magic left her body. It was as simple as that. She willed it, and so it was.

The pack began to whine, and one by one, each let out a howl, calling to the moon and their alpha, who was withering away before them. To break the sire bond, she had to let go of her immortality. She knew it, and he knew it, but deep down, Sheera had always been loyal to her people and no one else. Everything she'd done—bargaining with Eleanor all those years ago—she'd done for them.

The sound of a hundred wolves mourning the only alpha they'd ever known echoed around him, their despair rolling out across the forest. Nye sat next to Sheera, her silvery head resting in his lap. Stroking his fingers through the soft hair behind her ears, he waited, soothing her as the last of her life left the world and stepped into the next.

One by one, the pack turned their backs and disappeared through the trees, melting into the darkness until finally, he was alone with Sheera's body.

They would return once the moon had set, and they would take her for burial, but for now, the sky was her only company. The sky and Nye.

He couldn't blame her for what had happened tonight. Eleanor's poisonous stench was all over this. The Triskele's transformation was forced, he was sure of it, the immortality the wraith had given Sheera imbued with certain traits that gave her control over the wolf. They'd been played just as Nye and Isobel had.

He stood and cast one more look at the silver wolf, the mighty Triskele alpha, and disappeared into the trees.

He had to find Isobel.

Isobel powered down the stairs, her body covered in sweat and her lungs burning.

Sprinting through the empty castle, she fumbled in her bag for the car keys, positive she'd seen Nye drop them in when they'd arrived the previous day. It was well past midnight now, somewhere between the witching hour and sunrise, but it didn't matter. She was wide-awake and full of fear that almost blinded her.

If she were pregnant, then there was no way she was letting Eleanor get her slimy hands on her child. Nye's and her child.

As her fingers brushed against the keys, her heart skipped a beat in relief. Finding herself in the main entrance of the castle, she pushed against the front door and emerged out into the night. Now where did the car go? Spying it to the side of the driveway, she ran, her boots crunching on the gravel underfoot.

Pressing the button on the fob, the indicators flashed orange the locking mechanism disengaged. Yanking open the door, she threw her bag onto the back seat and slid behind the wheel.

Fumbling with the keys, she searched for the ignition but couldn't find it. Cursing, she realised it was a push-button start, and the key only had to be inside for it to work, so she jammed her finger on the button. Immediately, the engine turned over and began to purr.

Shoving the gearstick into drive, she glanced up and cried out, her heart twisting and her stomach flying into her throat. Of course, it wasn't going to be that easy. Just running out of the castle, not being stopped by anyone, and then driving off into the sunset. Stupid, naive, little Isobel!

Not ten meters in front of her stood the epic bitch known as Eleanor. Isobel didn't think it was possible to hate someone with as much pure loathing as she did right then, but she felt her veins burn. Why wouldn't she just piss the hell off already? What did she ever do to her?

Isobel's hands tightened around the steering wheel

as Eleanor's lips curved in triumph. She raised her hand, but Izzy wasn't waiting around to see what would happen. It was time to take the wraith down a peg or two. If she was knocked up with Nye's magical baby, there was no way in hell that bitch was getting her hands on it, no matter what it ended up being. It was hers and Nye's and no one else's baby. *A child was not a thing.*

"Bitch," Isobel cursed. "*Eat shit.*"

She slammed her foot on the accelerator, pushing it right to the floor. The car roared, the back tires spinning in the gravel. It fishtailed slightly to the left, and she eased up on the gas. It was enough to allow the tires to catch, and the car powered forward.

The split second before the hood collided with Eleanor, the wraith's eyes widened in surprise, then she slammed into the windshield, cracking the glass before sailing up over the roof.

Isobel didn't stop to see the carnage. She sped down the driveway and careened out onto the highway, almost smashing into a lorry. The driver blasted his horn as she righted the wheel, the tires screeching as her heart stuck in her throat.

She began to laugh hysterically, tears rolling down her face. *Holy shit!* Did she just run over Eleanor and live to tell the tale?

Her laughter soon turned into sobs as she drove, her heart twisting. Where was Nye? He said he would meet her on the road, but he was nowhere in sight as she settled the car into the left lane, her hands shaking and her stomach rolling. She had to keep going. He told her to keep going.

Realising she hadn't switched on the headlights, she turned the dial on the side of the steering wheel, and the road ahead was illuminated, the taillights of the lorry already disappearing off in the distance. The road was empty apart from her, and she kept driving, hoping she hadn't already passed Nye while she was freaking out.

When she was about five miles from the castle and almost losing hope he'd find her, a dark shape appeared ahead, arms waving. Recognising Nye—and hoping it wasn't a trick of her mind—she slowed and pulled off to the side. When the headlights lit up his familiar form, she heaved a sigh of relief and brought the car to a standstill, leaving the engine running.

He rounded the car and opened the driver's side, coaxing her to climb over the centre console.

"Are you okay?" he asked as she scurried into the passenger seat. "What happened to the windscreen?"

"Eleanor," she replied, grasping his arm to make sure he was really there and not a fear-induced hallucination. "I got in the car, started it, and she was standing in the driveway. I..."

"You ran her over?" he asked, his mouth falling open.

"What happened out there? Are the Triskele coming after us now, too?"

"No. They won't be a problem. Sheera's gone," he stated as he pulled the car back out onto the road. "Eleanor somehow used her immortality to embed some kind of control over her. The sire bond with the wolves ensured the pack would follow her every command."

"The Triskele were enslaved? All this time?"

Nye nodded. "Sheera sacrificed herself to save her pack. If anything, the Triskele have turned on the Unhallowed for what Eleanor did. They're back to changing with the moon, I'm afraid, but at least we won't have to worry about them coming for us. I hope."

So Sheera was only doing what she thought was right for her pack. Isobel could understand it to a point, but to live over four hundred years so they could escape the whims of the moon? She shook her head. There was too much left unsaid and even more that Nye had not explained to her. Her fingers found the pendant around her neck.

"Please, give me some answers," she said, her voice wavering. "After what just happened back there... I need some answers."

"Fine," he replied, his gaze never leaving the road. "That pendant I gave you was handed down from Triskele alpha to Triskele alpha until the day Sheera's father gave it to me. Free and clear." Nye's eyes blazed, his annoyance at an all-time high.

"A Triskele heirloom is stopping me from

becoming a wraith?" she asked, her breaths coming in short bursts. "Why'd he give it to you?"

"I saved his daughter," he said simply.

"Sheera?" Her mouth fell open.

"He had no sons, and she was his only offspring. I saved her while she was still a mortal wolf, and she went on to sacrifice herself to save them from the moon. The pendant was given to me as a sign of his gratitude, nothing more. It has no special powers. It's just a necklace."

"You could've just told me," Isobel exclaimed. "If it was that simple, why let me believe..." She trailed off.

"Because that day, I started something I never realised. Sheera believed she loved me, and I... I let her believe it when there was no hope."

"Because you loved Eleanor."

"I never loved her, either," he snapped.

"But you believed it at the time."

"What do you want me to say, Isobel?" he asked, his jaw tensing. "We're talking about something that happened four hundred years ago. I'm not the same man."

"I don't want you to say anything," she declared. "I only want to understand." She placed her hand over his, and his grasp tightened around the steering wheel. "You saved me back there. *Again.* You have nothing to prove. Not to me."

Silence opened up between them, the events of the night weighing heavily on both of them.

"What about the Triskele?" Isobel asked after a moment of reflection. "What will happen to them now?"

"Sheera's fate was sealed the day she accepted immortality from Eleanor," Nye replied. "There was never any saving her."

"So she's truly gone?"

"Nothing can live forever," he murmured, his eyes fixing on the road ahead. "Not even the immortal."

Chapter 10

G abby was waiting in the garage when the door opened, and the car carrying Nye and Isobel drove in.

She took one look at the cracked windshield, and her heart leapt. When she'd received a text message from Izzy saying they were on their way back, she hoped it was in one piece. By the looks of the car, they'd had one hell of a ride.

"You wouldn't believe the night we had," Isobel said, looking bedraggled as she got out of the car.

"What happened?" she asked, peering at the cracked windscreen. "Are you all right?"

"You were right, Gabby," Nye said as he threaded his arm through Isobel's arm. "Eleanor showed up and used the Triskele against us."

"The wolves came after you?"

"It's a long story." The spy shrugged as he led them

into the house. "Though I'm not sure your baby prediction was accurate."

"They didn't exactly have an opportunity to speak," Isobel said, heaving a sigh of relief the moment the garage door closed, and she was safely inside the manor. "Sheera was a wolf, and I ran Eleanor over. Smacked into the windscreen and flew off to bitchville as far as I'm concerned."

"You ran her over?" Gabby's mouth fell open, and she would have laughed, but it didn't seem appropriate considering the whole...*other* thing.

"Will you let me go?" Isobel snapped at Nye, wrenching her arm away. "I'm totally not pregnant."

Nye's grip loosened, and he glanced at Gabby with a worried look. If he was concerned...

"Pregnant?"

They all looked up as Alex appeared in the hallway, a confused look of anger on his face.

"It's not like that, Alex," Isobel said. "It's a bunch of bullshit if you ask me. I can't feel a thing."

"You usually can't," Nye muttered, drawing the wrath of the founder.

"Someone explain this to me?" Alex's eyes flashed. "A vampire knocked up my human sister?"

Isobel grasped his hand and tugged, turning his attention away from the vampire and onto her. "Let me explain..."

While the going was good, Gabby nudged Nye toward the stairs. An all-out brawl was the last thing she wanted to deal with, not when she was more desperate to hear what had happened with the Triskele.

Automatically, she led him toward the study, the room she felt most comfortable in. Memories of Regulus were all around, but they were mixed with those of her friends now, too. For lack of a better word, this place had become her home.

Flipping on the light, she crossed the room and flopped down into the armchair. She'd been up all night, worried sick about those two and the baby they'd probably made a few hours ago. A totally inappropriate picture appeared in her mind's eye, and she tried not to throw up. *Ugh.*

"Now tell me from the beginning," she said to the spy. "What was so important about the Triskele?"

"I explained this to Isobel already," he said. "She's wearing a Triskele heirloom, after all."

"It wasn't hard to notice something was up with it," Gabby said dryly. "Was it the alpha's?"

He shook his head. "Her father's."

"Okay, so not quite as bad but still awkward."

"The Triskele alpha is...was immortal," he began, ignoring her quip. Gabby sat up straight, suddenly more interested as he continued, "I've known her a long time. Sheera. I saved her from hunters as a child."

"Hunters? You mean she was changing when she was..."

Nye nodded. "She was in line to be the next alpha

even though she was a woman. Her transformations began earlier than others. I knew exactly what she was when I saw her. A little silver wolf. I saved her and took her back to her father, and he gifted me the pendant. I've kept it ever since."

"Sounds like you've known Sheera a lot through the years."

"She helped me escape the Unhallowed once or twice over the centuries."

"She made a bargain with Eleanor while she still held her human form. She wanted a way to stop her pack from turning with the moon. The Unhallowed gave her immortality, and it wasn't until last night that the catch was revealed." He shifted uneasily, and his head turned toward the door. The others must be coming. "Sheera's pack was bonded to her command. Eleanor forced her to transform, and the rest of the wolves had no choice but to follow. Through Sheera, the pack would have been enslaved."

"Would have?" Gabby asked with a frown.

"She broke the sire bond and gave up her immortality to save them from Eleanor."

Her eyebrows rose. The alpha sacrificed herself?

The door opened, and Alex stormed in, followed by a desperate looking Isobel.

"You say a vampire can't get a human pregnant?" he exclaimed, jabbing a finger at his sister. "Then listen!"

Nye stiffened, his eyes narrowing, but he took a wary step toward Isobel. Gabby watched closely as the spy's uncertainty was on full show. He didn't quite believe any of this was possible even though they'd witnessed some pretty crazy stuff.

Kneeling before Isobel, he placed his ear against her stomach, his hands grasping her slight waist. Then his eyes widened before screwing shut.

"How…" he whispered, staring up at a shocked looking Isobel. "It's only been hours."

Isobel glanced at Gabby. "There's a heartbeat. And my stomach is beginning to grow."

"Come here," she said, gesturing for her friend to sit in the other armchair.

Perching on the edge of hers, she placed her hands on Isobel's stomach and felt the significant bump for herself. Allowing a small tendril of power to flow through her palms and into Izzy's body, she felt what the other's had heard. The tiny thrum of a baby's heartbeat.

"They're right," she said. "There's definitely something in there."

"Something?" Isobel squeaked.

"If I may," she said. "I'm going to attempt to divine the baby's future."

"You can do that? But isn't it…not developed enough?"

"There's a heartbeat, Izzy," she murmured. "I'd say it's growing at a magical pace."

"I'm going to pop in days, not months?"

"Take a few deep breaths," she reassured her. "I'm

going to try to see."

Crossing to the other side was easy when it was only her mind that flew over the barrier. She slipped seamlessly into the stream, focusing her will on the little heartbeat.

Images flashed through her mind, thick and fast. Whoever the child was destined to be, there was going to be a great deal of power involved. The stream never flowed this quickly.

Reaching out, she attempted to grab something, *anything*, that might help her know who this child was meant to be and how she could help it.

The visions melted around her like silk, the cool touch of the other side chilling her bones and casting everything in a silver light. Finally, her fingers tightened around one, and she tore it away from the stream like a page from a book. Instantly, her mind was assaulted by an image so bright and colourful she almost pulled out of the stream and returned to the land of the living.

A little girl stared at her, the spitting image of Isobel, but as soon as she beheld it, she was flung backward, her connection severed.

Gabby's eyes opened, and she knew. The baby was a little girl, but beyond that, it was anyone's guess.

What did Eleanor want with the baby? She knew it would have the power necessary to resurrect the Unhallowed, but it would take time to train the child. Years, in fact. Would it be sacrificed? The thought of the poor little thing being used in such a terrible way made her feel sick.

Eleanor mustn't get her hands on Isobel and Nye's child.

"What did you see?" Isobel asked as Gabby pulled her hands away.

She watched her friend closely, knowing her witchy ways caused her to speak in riddles most often than not. If there was any time she needed things laid out clearly, it was now.

"It's a little girl," she muttered, looking troubled.

"A girl?" Nye asked, his voice sounding far away.

Isobel's stomach churned, her gaze drawn to the window where beyond the sun was rising. Not even a day had passed, and she was going to be a mother?

Voices hummed in her ears, but nothing was registering. Panic began to set in, nausea rising in uncontrollable waves. A few weeks ago, her biggest problem had been her thesis, and now she was going to be a mother to a miracle baby whose father was a four-hundred-year-old vampire? She couldn't handle it. This was way too much.

"If Eleanor engineered this…" she began haltingly. "Is any of this child mine? Is it…"

"It's yours and Nye's," Gabby said, taking her hands. "It's none of her."

"But... She needs a witch. I'm only human."

"That's what the curse was for," Gabby explained. "She made you one. You don't have any powers, but she gave you her witch's essence so you could pass on the legacy."

"The pendant..." Her hand flew to her neck. "So I'm not becoming a wraith?"

"You'll still need to wear it, I'm afraid. It was rash of Eleanor to curse you the way she did."

"Why?"

"She was banking on me being able to find a way to halt the effects. Just as she was hoping Nye would turn himself over to her the night of the ritual."

"I'm glad I ran over her, then," Isobel declared. "I know she isn't dead, but I hope she's got one hell of a headache."

Nye knelt beside her, looking just as frightened as she was. She supposed he didn't bank on this happening, either. They'd been played in the most conniving way possible.

"Where's Tristan?" the spy asked. "We need to step up our defence of the manor. Eleanor was a hair's breadth from taking her."

Silence descended on the room, and Isobel suddenly felt guilty. She hadn't had a chance to tell him Tristan had left two days ago now. There hadn't really been time what with freaking out over impossible babies, being hunted by werewolves, and being cornered by a psychopathic wraith.

"Hello?" Nye exclaimed, glancing around the room. "I spoke out loud, didn't I?"

"Tristan's gone," Gabby said after a moment. "He left the night before Isobel's relapse."

"What a coincidence," the spy drawled, glaring at the witch. "Eleanor was able to reactivate the curse, and obviously, she waved her magic wand and summoned her man-servant."

"No, I won't believe it," she hissed. "He left because he felt like he was a danger to us all. He believed that if Eleanor could get to him so easily, she could do it again. He didn't want to cause any more harm."

"I think he thought she could ignite her compulsion the same way as my curse," Isobel mused, laying her hand on Nye's shoulder.

"How would he have known?" Alex asked. "We didn't until the next day."

"I don't know," she declared. "He was very old and wise like a vampire Yoda. Perhaps he sensed it. It doesn't matter anyway. He's gone."

"Why are you so upset about it?" Nye asked, rising to his feet. "He was a stick in the mud."

She turned on him, her eyes blazing. "He helped me, Nye. When you were too busy ignoring me, your burdensome human prisoner, he was the one who made sure I had food. You know, the stuff that keeps puny humans alive? If you don't eat, you don't shit. And if you don't shit, you die."

His eyebrow rose. "How poignant."

"We have to go on without him," Alex said. "You have an entire city at your beck and call, Nye. Use it."

"It's not that simple," the spy said, grinding his teeth.

"It is," Gabby declared. "If the Unhallowed are resurrected, then it's *everyone's* problem."

Isobel listened to her friends bickering, and her stomach gurgled. A million questions echoed through her head, none of them having to do with fortifying the manor or tracking down a way to kill a wraith for good. They had everything to do with how fast this baby was growing and if she'd be alive at the end of it.

Rising to her feet, her head swam, and her brow prickled with sweat. What if she didn't make it out the other end? What if she died giving birth to this little girl? *Her* little girl. What if all this was for nothing?

"I'm going to be sick," she exclaimed, then rushed from the study, aiming straight for the bathroom in her bedroom.

Sliding on the tiled floor, she made just in time. Nye was beside her in an instant, gently pulling her hair behind her back as she popped, the contents of her stomach emptying into the toilet bowl.

"If this ain't true love, then fucked if I know what it is," he muttered, rubbing her back.

All Isobel could do was moan in reply.

Chapter 11

When Isobel woke, it was dark outside. She must have slept the entire day away.

Rolling onto her side, she gasped when she felt the size of her stomach. It was the size of a basketball!

"That's really something," Nye said beside her.

"Don't sound so smug," she bit out as he came into focus. "You put it there."

"I heard no complaining."

Pushing up, she sat beside the vampire, and her heart bloomed with a sharp burst of love. Every emotion under the sun wove a path through her, but that was the one she had to focus on. She didn't know how long he'd been sitting beside her on the bed, but she was glad he was there when she'd woken. Especially since she was still coming to terms with the turbo baby in her guts.

"I'm worried," she whispered, laying her head on his shoulder.

"About what?" His arm circled around her back, and his chilled body temperature began to cool her fevered brow.

"*Everything.*"

He smoothed his other hand through her hair. "It's going to be fine."

She pouted. "How do you know?"

"Faith," he retorted. "And the fact I know you."

She squirmed against him. "Oh, you know me now?"

"We haven't had a great deal of time together," he replied with a chuckle, "but I know who you are. That's more important right now than knowing what your favourite movie is. Or your favourite colour. Or if you're a salty or sweet person."

"Salty or sweet?"

"Sweet," he said, kissing the top of her head. "Definitely sweet. Do you remember the million pounds of chocolate you requested that time?"

"Do I ever. The look on your face when I said I needed tampons was hilarious. I'll never forget the blind panic."

"I tried to send Tristan..." he began but fell silent at the mention of the knight's name.

"He'll come back," she murmured, knowing the old vampire had come to mean more to Nye than he'd ever likely admit. "When he's ready."

He grunted and held her tighter.

Letting out a yawn, Isobel clutched his shirt. "You're a big softy at heart, you know that?"

"I think you're delirious," he quipped, easing her back down onto the bed.

"I think you're avoiding the truth."

He smiled. "Nope."

"You want the world to see you as a tough guy, but I know better. The moment this little girl comes into the world, you're going to melt like butter."

Nye shook his head in amusement and kissed her swiftly on the lips.

"Sleep," he said. "We need you well rested, love."

"We?"

"Me and her." He nodded at her stomach.

"See, I told you," she said as her eyes drooped. "You're a big softy."

———

The next day dawned bright, and finally, Isobel woke with a calm mind.

Nye was nowhere to be seen, but she didn't expect him to fawn over her twenty-four seven. He was probably off someplace working out a plan to kill Eleanor once and for all. Or at least she hoped he was.

Rubbing her hands over her belly, she stilled as she saw how fat she'd grown overnight. She kind of expected it, but her heart began to beat double time as her hands probed the hard bulge that used to be a very flat and trim waistline, gained by years of substandard meals while buried under a mound of books in the Oxford University library.

Sliding awkwardly out of bed, Isobel dragged her bloated body into the bathroom. Staring at herself in the mirror, her mouth fell open in panic. She looked a lot bigger than she felt. Turning to the side, she inspected her profile, and her throat tightened in alarm.

She was growing faster than she should, so why did she feel fine? Besides the odd bout of morning sickness, she hadn't experienced any discomfort. Well, only when she looked down.

Peering into her eyes, she poked at the lack of dark circles under her eyes and didn't know what to do. Shouldn't there be something she ought to be doing? Didn't pregnant woman take birthing classes, down special vitamins, and eat weird things? Shouldn't she have heartburn and want to pee all the time? Something other than blowing up like a balloon should be happening.

Beginning to panic, she threw on a dressing gown and cursed when it wasn't even big enough to cover her stomach. Leaving it open, she made do with one of Nye's T-shirts underneath, which was stretched taught, and her usual pyjama bottoms that she could only pull up half as far as usual. If she twisted the wrong way, it would be a comedy of errors.

She found Gabby in the study.

"Gabby," she said as she waddled into the study. "I expanded again."

The witch glanced up from her grimoire and the spell she was conjuring on the surface of the desk. She took one look at Isobel's stomach, and her eyes widened.

"I'll say," she said, her spell forgotten. "Are you feeling okay?"

"That's the thing. Other than a bit of puking, I'm fine. That's not natural, right? Two days in and I'm like four months pregnant. Not that I know what it's meant to look like. All I know is I'm probably going to pop in a couple of days. *Days, Gabby!* This shit is meant to take months, and now I've got hours to prepare myself for being a mother to a magical baby none of us knows a thing about."

"Izzy, you need to calm down."

"I can't calm down! I'm going to squeeze a baby out of my vagina. A week ago, my biggest problem was worrying why Nye didn't want to kiss me and now... *Well, he kissed me all right!*"

"Sit down before you fall over," the witch said, practically dragging her to one of the armchairs by the fireplace.

Sinking down onto the leather, Isobel sighed loudly. "What's happening to me, Gabby?"

"The curse must have altered your body," she mused. "In order to withstand the fast growth of the baby, there must've been some tampering with your natural form..."

"That doesn't sound good," Isobel muttered, wiping her palm across her forehead.

"Eleanor was meant to bear the child herself," Gabby went on. "She must've planned this spell in meticulous detail. Changing one thing would cause it to unravel, and she would have to redo everything."

"Then she used the same one on me, delivered by the curse. She would've had to be alive afterward to help the child grow into her powers, right? Then that means I'll get through this. Right?"

Gabby didn't look as excited as she felt, and her hopes began to fade.

"The only person who knows for sure is Eleanor," she said. "And she's not fond of talking."

"Only taking," Isobel whispered. "She'll come soon, right?"

Gabby nodded, her gaze falling to Isobel's enlarged stomach, which began to squirm, followed by a sharp pain on her left side.

"Ow!" Isobel said, wincing. Her hands flew to her stomach, and the squirming came again, but this time, a little softer.

"What is it?" Gabby asked, kneeling before her.

Isobel's eyes widened, and her fear subsided, replaced by wonder as she realised her little girl was waking up. "I think she's kicking."

The witch placed her hands on Isobel's stomach and smiled as the little girl sank her foot in again.

"Bloody hell!" Gabby exclaimed. "She's got a bit of strength in her."

"It's going to be okay," Isobel whispered, more to the baby than to herself. "Everything is going to be okay. I know it."

Gabby stood beside the olive tree in the garden, watching the sunrise through the branches.

Regulus's remains were buried under its roots, the tree she'd grown herself the night they'd laid her lover to rest. Sometimes, she imagined she could feel his presence if she concentrated her earth sense hard enough, but she knew she wasn't really feeling anything. Her imagination was strong in those moments, tricking even her. Even with all her power and abilities, she couldn't talk to all of the dead. Katrin had told her as much when she'd spoken to the founding witch on the other side. He'd gone someplace even she couldn't reach.

If there was any time she needed his council, it was now.

The baby had grown at a pace none of them had anticipated. Isobel's stomach had doubled in size each day, her body hardly keeping up with the accelerated pregnancy. Would her friend survive the birth?

A shuffling sound alerted her to a presence, and she glanced over her shoulder. Reed stood behind her, his hands jammed into the pockets of his leather jacket.

Gabby narrowed her eyes and turned her attention back to the olive tree, but he didn't take the hint. He stood beside her and watched the sunrise, annoying with all his young vampire hotness.

Finally, Reed glanced at her. "You good?"

"Of course, I am," she retorted.

"Hey, just asking," he said, holding up his hands in mock defence. "Everyone's fussing over Isobel. Understandably, since she's full up with the baby plague, but no one's asked you if you're dealing." Gabby eyed him with suspicion, but he went on, oblivious to her concern. "You're the one who's going to swoop in and save the day. Magic always trumps all, or so they say. That's gotta be heavy."

"You're cocky," she said, turning to face him. "Lurking around the manor, eavesdropping on conversations you're not privy to. You know more than you're supposed to." She allowed her power to hum, the air charging around her. "Don't you think it's time you explain yourself before I jump to conclusions?"

"What kind of conclusions might they be?"

"That you're in league with Eleanor. Perhaps not willingly, but you never know."

Reed snorted and shook his head.

"Or there's the fact that Tristan's gone missing. I

believe he left of his own accord, but that doesn't mean you never found him. Are we going to find him strung up somewhere with a rune carved onto his desiccated body? Or should we set another place at the table when he rolls up all zombified?"

"You have one hell of an imagination," Reed said with a laugh. "I can see why you're so jumpy. It's admirable."

"Admirable?"

"Yeah, the way you protect your friends despite your differences." He glanced at the sky, which was streaked with brilliant shades of red and orange. "It would be nice to be part of something like that. I've spent a lot of time...*wandering*."

Gabby watched him closely, her magic flowing around the humanoid and into the earth of its own accord. She didn't have to listen to the emotions feeding back to her to understand she was wrong. Reed wasn't their enemy. He just wanted to be a part of something.

"I wouldn't mind being a part of this place. London. I've been watching and listening, not because I want to do you harm but in case I was needed. I have all time in the world. Too much, in fact."

"Is that the only reason?" she asked, sensing he was holding back.

He grunted.

"You seem to know everything while I know

nothing. Nye trusts you on reputation alone, but that's not enough. Not anymore."

"No matter what I do, no matter how hard I fight, I'm still on the outside," he said, his scowl deepening. "How many more times do I need to pledge my allegiance?"

"Don't you think it's time you give me the whole story?" she asked, thoroughly annoyed at his constant evasion. He was angry? Well, so was she.

He ground his teeth together, his jaw tightening, and he turned away from her.

"*Reed*," she snapped.

"I never met my father," he said after a moment. "I was still in my mother's belly when he went off to war. He never came back. I don't even know if he knew I existed. Not for a long time." He sighed, his shoulders rising and falling. "I grew up with my mother and my older sister, knowing my father had gone off to fight in a pointless war. It was truly shit knowing that, but it was what it was. Nothing I could do would change the fact he was gone."

"I'm sorry," Gabby murmured, beginning to feel rotten she'd threatened the vampire.

"What they say about vampires is true," he went on. "The most defining moments of your human life follow you to the grave."

She didn't have to ask him to know one of his moments was his father's death.

"For a very long time, I thought he was dead," Reed

went on. "It wasn't until I became a vampire that I learned he still lived."

"He was alive?"

"Is," he replied, turning to face her.

"What do you mean?" she asked. "He's…"

"Reed isn't my real name," he said, looking worried.

"Then what is it?" Gabby's hackles rose, hoping this wasn't going to be bad. The last thing she needed was another conspiracy that could tear them apart. One was more than enough.

Reed cast his gaze away and swallowed hard. "Aedan na Tri Tor."

Gabby's heart skipped about a thousand beats. "You're…"

"Tristan's son."

"But that would mean…"

"I'm nearing my nine-hundred-and-eighty-something birthday. Give or take a few years. It's hard to keep up." He raised an eyebrow and smirked at her. "Try sticking that many candles in a cake."

Gabby stepped forward, no longer suspicious of the vampire's intentions. Placing her hand on his arm, she drew his gaze back to hers. "Why didn't you say anything? All this time, you've been working by his side in the Six…"

"I was afraid, I suppose. He never knew me." He shrugged. "After a billion years, you'd think I'd have a handle on that shit."

Feeling his anguish, she attempted to soothe him with her power, but he shook her away.

"Now he's gone, and he's not coming back," he went on. "It took me a thousand years to find him...it can't take me a thousand more."

"Stand with us," Gabby said, taking his hands. "Stand with us, Reed. Tristan's coming back. I know it."

"Your words are stronger than your conviction," he said wryly.

"Reed, please."

He stared at her for a long time, his gaze studying her features in minute detail. Just as things were beginning to get awkward, he smiled.

"Where else would I go?"

Chapter 12

Nye stood on the balcony overlooking the garden and scowled at Gabby.

She'd taken to sitting underneath Regulus's olive tree night and day for unknown reasons, and that was where he found her, yet again. She sat cross-legged and still as a statue, her mind someplace else. The sun was setting, and the garden was alive with every shade of red and orange his vampire eyes could discern. It was a pretty scene, and Isobel would enjoy taking it in if she were here with him, but he had no heart for it.

Five days had passed since he'd escaped the Triskele with Isobel, and the baby's growth hadn't slowed. Of all the messed up things he'd been through, this had to be the worst. He was undead, the leader of the London vampires, and nowhere near father material. How was he meant to raise a child among all the day-to-day carnage that was his life?

He was taking things far worse than Isobel, and she was the one who was pregnant. She'd just picked herself up and gotten on with it, knowing she couldn't change her fate. She had to, so she did. There was no other recourse, but for Nye...he struggled with it more than he wanted to admit.

Babies did nothing but sleep, eat, and cry, not to mention shit like it was going out of fashion. What did he know about children? Nothing at all. If anyone knew how to change a nappy, it was Tristan na Tri Tor, but he'd run while the going was good. Could he run right along with him? No. It was impossible. He was bound to Isobel with or without a child in tow.

Narrowing his eyes at Gabby, he wondered if she was running in her own way. Creating other worlds in her mind in an attempt to switch off because she didn't know what to do about Eleanor, either.

The wraith would come for the baby, plucking the infant from her mother's arms the moment she was born. It was cruel and callous, but to the Unhallowed, it was just a thing. The power it held would be used, and once the child had served its purpose...

No, Nye couldn't run from this. Isobel would be devastated, and the child... Who knew what would become of it...*her*.

Gabby stirred and glanced over her shoulder. She scanned the yard, sensing she was being watched, and after a moment, she caught his gaze. Knowing she would seek him out if he didn't speak to her now, he vaulted over the balustrade, hopped onto the roof, and leapt to the ground, hardly denting the grass.

"Show off," the witch said as she got to her feet.

"What are you doing?" he asked with a scowl.

"Communing," she retorted. "What? Did you think I was skipping out on you?"

"Yes."

She snorted. "Unlikely. I've been trying to speak to the ancestor spirits, but they've been elusive these past few days."

Nye rolled his eyes. "Why? Are they pissed a vampire procreated?"

"I'd say so," she replied, completely serious. "But it isn't anyone but the Unhallowed's fault. The problem is convincing them. They see things as very black and white. You made the baby, so you're at fault even though you were tricked. It's very annoying, to be honest."

"Believe me, it's the last thing I expected. I was more worried about biting her again than all of this."

"And do you want to?" the witch asked. "Bite her?"

"I'll always want to," he replied thinly. "It's my nature, but I can control it better than I thought."

He sighed and glanced up at the manor to where the windows of Isobel's room looked down over where they stood. She was human with no supernatural abilities, and yet she had the most conviction of all of them. How was that possible? Isobel's heart was stronger than even he understood.

"And the baby?" Gabby asked, drawing his attention back down to earth.

"What about it?"

"What will you do once she's born? It won't be long now. Maybe two or three days."

He shrugged. Her guess was as good as his.

"You're welcome to stay at the manor for as long as you need."

Nye scowled for what felt like the hundredth time in the last five minutes and turned to face the witch. "What's that supposed to mean? We don't even know what she is. Not for sure. Shit, we don't even know if we can fight off Eleanor. Once the baby is born, it could be the end of everything. Why plan for an uncertain future?"

Gabby shook her head and glanced at the olive tree. "Because a life without hope is no life at all."

Nye's shoulders tensed, but he nodded his understanding. After all the things he'd been through, he had to believe this would work out. Sheera had died in his arms only a few nights ago, and Isobel was about to give birth. He had to be strong despite his uncertainty. Isobel was unfaltering in her courage, after all.

"I'll get them to talk to me," Gabby went on. "We still have time."

"Not much of it."

He heard Isobel's voice on the air, the sound faint and muffled, but she was calling his name. Without a second glance or a single word, he left Gabby to her communing. What could he do to help her? Nothing since the ancestor spirits hated his guts merely because he was a vampire. Good luck to them.

A life without hope...

Gabby watched Nye disappear back into the house.

He was struggling more with the realisation he was going to become a father than their lack of power to fight Eleanor. He feared for the child even as he struggled with his responsibility.

Settling back onto the grass, she stared up at the olive tree. What would Regulus do? He would chip away at the problem until it crumbled in his hands, that's what he would do. Perhaps she needed to take more of a head-on approach and stop being so darn polite all the time.

It was risky. The spirits might stop talking to her totally if she pushed too hard, but she'd done nothing but appease their wishes from the first moment they'd spoken to her. Gabby was more than a vessel to exact their will on the living. She was not their tool just as the child would not be one for Eleanor.

Closing her eyes, she focused her earth sense and felt out the edges of the veil that separated the land of the living from the other side. She'd had a great deal of practice over the last few months, having communed with Katrin and the other spirits who resided deep within the mists. The cool tendrils of the spirit realm tickled against her skin, and she opened her eyes, slipping through the curtain with expert precision.

"Hey!" she yelled into the silvery void. "Hey, you! It's Gabrielle Cohen, remember me? The witch you hide from every time I knock on the door."

Nothing answered her angry call.

"*Hey!* I'm talking to you!"

Nothing.

"Oh, so when you want me to do your dirty work, you're all chatty, but when the world hangs on the brink and I need your help for a change, you're nowhere to be seen! Well, that's just selfish. The all-powerful ancestor spirits. *Pfft! Pathetic.*"

A hum began to sound in her ears, the mist beginning to shimmer.

"Come on!" she went on. "Strike me down, or help me save the world from a coven of scum sucking wraiths. *You know you want to!*"

"*Silence!*"

Gabby stilled as the veil shimmered, the mist swirling in violent gusts as the silhouette of a woman emerged, gaining strength and form until she stood before her.

"Who..." she began, but as the woman reached out and brushed her fingers against Gabby's cheek, understanding flooded her mind.

Ismena.

One of the five founding witches. She was of the ether, which meant she was standing before her ancestor, the beginning of her bloodline. Over two thousand years ago, she'd been gifted her abilities by a Celestine named Ayasti—Aya, the Witch Hunter's, mother.

"Ismena?" Gabby whispered in shock.

"You have my attention, Gabrielle. Speak."

"How..."

"I am here with great difficulty on my part," she replied. "My essence has retreated far into the ether, so touching the lives of the living is not the easiest task."

"I need your help," she began. "The Unhallowed..."

"Yes, I know of them," Ismena replied. "These creatures, these Unhallowed wraiths, must not be allowed to return to the living."

"I know," Gabby said. "We've been trying to find a way to sever their ties, but nothing... I can't find a way and now..."

Ismena pursed her lips. "The child."

"Is that why you won't talk to me? You must understand," Gabby pleaded. "They were tricked. The only crime they're guilty of is love."

"He is a vampire. He is preying on an innocent human woman. The people we are sworn to protect."

"Nye never wanted to become a vampire. He was forced like many who have come before and after. He'll be a good father to this child and protect her with his life. There's goodness in him. I've seen it."

"You fell in love with Regulus," Ismena went on. "The Roman who pledged his allegiance to Katrin, the Betrayer."

"The world is not black and white!" Gabby cried, her heart twisting. "You're accusing me of betraying my people when I have done nothing but sacrifice myself to fight for them! I've lost more than I ever had, I've protected those who have had their human lives taken from them, and I've protected and fought with the last of the Celestines! I've given so much, and now that I'm asking for a little bit of help, you won't give it?" Tears began to stream down her face as the frustration she'd locked inside for the last few months burst forth. "You force your will on me and expect me to jump without asking why, and I've jumped, no questions asked. I need help! *Please*..."

"There..." The veil parted, the edges shimmering around the spirit's form. "Do you hear that?"

Gabby sniffed, brushing away her tears. "Hear what?"

"The sound of your conviction. You love them despite what they are."

"I love them for *who* they are," she said defiantly.

The founder smiled, and the veil shimmered.

"The child is the key," Ismena said, cupping Gabby's cheek in her palm.

At her touch, light burst through Gabby's mind, and suddenly, she understood. It wasn't a mere witch with power Eleanor needed. No, it was much more than that.

Isobel was a human imbued with a witch legacy. Nye was a vampire who had immortality. Their child would be a hybrid of the two, which meant a fusing of their abilities.

A truly *immortal witch*.

Unlimited power. Unlimited knowledge. No training necessary. This child would be the most powerful supernatural creature *ever*. This was how the Unhallowed would be resurrected.

Eleanor had planned to carry the child herself all those years ago, but the moment that Nye killed her human body and cursed her to becoming a wraith was the moment the last of the Unhallowed were rendered infertile.

Nye was the seed, Eleanor was the bearer, and the child—the immortal witch—was the fruit of their salvation.

"Now you understand," Ismena said, her musical voice floating through the veil. "She is unnatural. What happens in her first moments of life will determine who she will be. Light or dark. Guide her, Gabrielle."

Holding out her palm, Ismena gestured to her.

Leaning forward, she gasped as she beheld a perfect diamond teardrop against the founding witch's silver skin.

"My gift to the child. May it bring her light when all others go out."

Gabby plucked the jewel from Ismena's palm as the veil began to shimmer, and the world began to come back into view around her. The outline of the witch blurred, fading until it was no more. Finally, she was alone in the garden, the olive tree towering above her.

Uncurling her hand, Gabby stared down at the teardrop and understood what they had to do. It was the only way they could defeat the Unhallowed for good. The child was the key.

If Eleanor got her hands on the baby the moment she was born, then she would be guided to the dark, and all would be lost. With no way of stopping the wraith, there was only one course of action. Protect Isobel and the baby at all costs.

Besides, they had one thing up their sleeve Eleanor hadn't counted on.

The love of a mother.

By halting the spread of the curse, Isobel would bear the child as a human, not a potential wraith as Eleanor had been before she'd died.

Turning, she found Isobel sitting on a bench on the patio, her gaze studying the sky, which had turned dark while Gabby had been on the other side. The first stars of the night were already shining through, the lights of London dulling their brilliance.

"Hey," Gabby said, shuffling up the stairs, her feet thudding on the flagstones.

"I didn't want to disturb you," Isobel replied. "You looked so calm."

"I was communing with the ancestor spirits," she explained. "They've been elusive these past few days, but I finally got them to talk."

"Yeah?" Isobel straightened as much as her enormous belly would allow. "What did they say?"

"Well, they're pretty angry about the baby, but that was always going to be a given."

Izzy scowled and smoothed her palms over her stomach. "What did she do to anyone?"

"Nothing. She's a victim just as much as any of us, but she's unnatural."

"If the bloody spirits are pissed at anyone, it should be Eleanor and her cronies."

Uncurling her hand, Gabby stared down at the teardrop Ismena had gifted her. They definitely were.

"She was trying to turn you into a wraith," she said, voicing her thoughts. "To ensure the child was born to darkness."

"She was trying to turn me into one of those soul-sucking leeches after all?" She collapsed back onto the bench, her belly bulging. "*Bloody hell.*"

"We stopped it," Gabby said, sitting beside her.

"As long as I wear the Triskele's pendant, then I'll be fine. I can handle that." She glanced at her stomach.

"The child is..." She sighed, not knowing how to explain it.

"Is what, Gabby?"

"She'll be an immortal witch. Prone to both light and dark. Her first moments of life will determine the course of her eternity."

Isobel began to shake. "*What?*"

"If she remains with you and Nye, then I have no doubt in my mind she'll turn to the light. Love, laughter, happiness...kindness. Those are the things she needs."

"And if Eleanor gets her greasy mitts on her, then she'll become just as twisted." Isobel rubbed her eyes. "Hear that, baby? Mommy loves you with all the sunshine and rainbows in the world."

At that moment, her friend's strength was insurmountable. With Isobel as her mother, the child would only have one path to follow, and that would be to the light. Goodness flowed through every fibre of her body.

"I can handle a lot of things," Izzy went on, "like immortal wolves, vampire sex, curses being stopped by a werewolf heirloom and witch spirits, but what I can't handle is the fact an immortal witch is growing in my womb. It's been a week, and I'm already on the verge of popping!"

They fell into silence as the gravity of their

situation sank in. There was nothing else they could say about it.

"Gabby..." Isobel began uneasily. "Am I going to make it through this? I know I've been fine so far, but what if the moment she's born... What if my body..."

"Don't say that."

"It's a possibility, right?"

"No, I won't allow it. The baby needs you to guide her."

She grasped her friend's arm. "Gabby, I'm scared. I told Nye I was fine, but I..." She held her stomach. "I want to be around to help her. She needs a mother. I want to protect her, but..."

"No buts," Gabby said firmly. "I'll do whatever it takes to make sure you get to see her grow up." She held out her palm, showing the jewel to Isobel. "Ismena gave this to me. A gift for the baby."

"Ismena?"

"The founder of my bloodline," she explained. "She was the one who helped me. This is one of her tears. A light when all others go out, she said."

Isobel stared at the jewel for a long time before she nodded and glanced away. Placing her hand on her stomach, she smiled. "I think she likes it."

Gabby closed her hand around the teardrop and focused her will, warming and shaping until she felt her intention completely manifest. When she held out the jewel for her friend, she smiled at the creation.

The diamond was entwined with strands of spun

silver, the point shimmering as if it'd been dipped in a pot of liquid magic, the tip left open with space for a chain to be threaded through.

"Keep it close," Gabby murmured, handing it to Isobel. "Once she's born..."

Izzy nodded, closing her hand around the pendant. Like mother like daughter.

Chapter 13

Day seven of babygeddon dawned, and Isobel was beginning to feel like a stuffed chicken.

Her feet were swollen, her bladder was squashed, she was eating like a horse, and she'd forgotten the last time she'd washed her hair. It was a wonder Nye didn't plug his nose when he was around her. Honestly, she wondered why he'd stuck around at all. She was a mess.

If there was any blessing to their current situation, it was the fact Eleanor had gone silent. Isobel wondered if it meant she'd smashed the wraith up real good when she hit her with the car, but Isobel knew she was hoping for too much.

Desperate for some fresh air, Isobel decided to go out into the garden. The wards Gabby had placed around the grounds would alert them of trouble long before it arrived, so the thought of sitting out in the open didn't bother her as much as it probably should. Besides, the way the baby squirmed when the sunlight hit her belly made her believe she liked the sunshine, too.

Out in the hall, she could hear Nye's muffled voice inside the study, but she didn't open the door. Leaving him in peace so he could run his kingdom, she waddled down the stairs—taking about a million years to descend—shuffled through the kitchen, and opened the back door.

Instantly, the sweet scent of lilac wafted up her nose, and she smiled. Her senses seemed sharper since she'd gotten knocked up, if that was even possible. She supposed her hormones were in overdrive with the week-long stomach explosion, or it could be the fact she was growing an immortal witch.

Stepping outside, she sat on the bench and shielded her eyes from the summer sun, staring at the view of London over the tops of the trees. The manor sat on a rise, and on a clear day, she imagined she could see the outline of the Shard, the tallest building in the whole city.

Her thoughts wandered as she relaxed. If they got out of this, what would she do then? Her dream of traveling the world and finishing her Masters had been flung out of the window in the most dramatic fashion, her plans on digging up half the ancient world crumbling into ashes. Maybe she could still do those things, but what would Nye want to do? He was the leader of the London vampires. He wouldn't be able to go anywhere.

Then there was the baby.

Maybe she would know what to do once the baby was born. People said things just clicked the moment their kids came into the world. Maybe it would be the same for her.

The air crackled like a bug slapping into an electronic zapper and frying to a crisp. *Zap!* Her heart leapt, and her shoulders stiffened, realising it must be one of the wards reacting to someone crossing the boundary. She had to get back indoors and tell Nye.

Rising to her feet, she cursed her awkwardness. Damn, she was so top-heavy it was a wonder she hadn't fallen on her ass already.

Before she could step into the kitchen, a man stepped onto the patio, and she let out a yelp, but there was no need to be afraid. She recognised Tristan immediately. *He'd come back!*

"Isobel?" he asked, his Irish accent sounding thicker—if that were even possible. His confused gaze fell to her stomach.

"Tristan? Where have you been? We've been worried about you!" She took a step toward him, relief flooding through her body.

"Really?" he asked with a shake of his head.

"Of course!"

Before she could take another step, Nye appeared out of thin air and collided with the knight. The two vampires sailed over the edge of the patio and flew across the yard, tumbling over the turf before righting themselves.

"*Nye!*" Isobel cried, rushing forward. "What do you think you're doing?"

"Coward," the spy snarled at the knight. "What an opportune time to show up."

He took a swing at Tristan, his fist slamming into his cheekbone with a thud that echoed across the garden. Isobel winced, her own cheek throbbing in sympathy, but the knight hardly moved, let alone blinked.

"You had better start explaining yourself, Tristan na Tri Tor, or I won't be so gentle next time."

Isobel's mouth fell open. That punch was gentle? The force behind that would have broken any normal man's cheekbone! She wondered if she'd ever understand vampires, let alone the way their bodies healed within seconds.

"I went to see Arrow," Tristan said, rubbing his cheek.

"Aya?" Nye exclaimed, throwing his hands into the air. "You expect me to believe that?"

"If anyone could help me with my compulsion, it was her."

"So you don't trust Gabby now? *She removed it.*"

"I couldn't trust myself," he said, his voice beginning to rise. "I couldn't live with the betrayal."

Abruptly, he fell to his knees, his head bowed in submission.

Isobel glanced at Nye, her eyes wide and her heart breaking. What was Tristan doing? Was he offering his life to Nye? Did he want to die? She didn't understand what was happening.

"Is that what you want?" Nye drawled, sounding bored. "You want me to put an end to a thousand years of your pathetic suffering?"

"Stop it!" Isobel declared, moving across the grass as fast as she could manage. "Leave him alone!"

Nye glanced at her with a raised eyebrow. "Go inside," he commanded. "You don't want to see this."

"Like hell, I will," she replied, jutting out her chin. "Leave him the hell alone."

"This is none of your business, Isobel."

"How dare you!" she cried at the spy. "How dare you dismiss me after all we've been through."

"This is vampire business," he said, grasping her shoulders. "You're not part of this."

"Like hell." She scoffed and hugged her belly. "This is family business. Stuff being a vampire."

Nye hesitated, his brow creasing in confusion. "Is that really how you see him?"

"*Duh!*" She shoved past him and stood before Tristan, who hadn't moved an inch. "Being stuffed with a magical baby on fast forward makes you see things *real clear like.* I won't let you hurt him, Nye."

Tristan's head was still lowered in submission, his

hair hiding his face from her. Knowing there was no hope in hell she was getting up off the ground if she sat down, she nudged the knight with her foot.

"Get up, for goodness sake," she said, rolling her eyes. "No one is dying today." When he didn't move, she declared, "Don't make me get down there because I'm so not getting up on my own. I want to keep some dignity, you know, and rolling around like a bloody beached whale won't help."

"Isobel—"

"Shut up," she hissed at Nye, who took a step back as she tugged at Tristan's shoulder. "How about *you* go inside for a change? I'm not one of your royal subjects, *your highness*."

Nye scowled and turned away, seeming to know what was good for him. Once he'd gone, she threaded her arm through the knight's as he finally stood.

"There. Isn't that better?" she declared.

Tristan nodded, looking sheepish. "Isobel—"

"Shush, he'll come around," she said kindly as she allowed him to escort her into the house. "It's been a rough couple of weeks." She waved her hand toward the garden behind them. "All of that won't help anyone."

They found themselves in the sitting room, and she sank onto the sofa, the soft fabric feeling heavenly against her aching limbs. Tristan sat beside her, his gaze fixed on her enormous stomach. Talk about the elephant in the room.

"It seems I have missed a great deal," he said, warily. "Is it a boy or a girl?"

"A girl," she said proudly, the emotion startling her. She supposed he was rather used to the idea now.

"Her heart is strong," he commented.

"You can hear it?"

He nodded. "It's a strange thing to see after being away for such a short amount of time. I'm beginning' to wonder if more time has passed and I've..."

"No," she said firmly. "It's only been a week since I caught the baby plague." When the knight raised his eyebrows, she added, "That line is courtesy of Reed, bless him."

"He's still here?"

She nodded. "Hasn't left. He's been helping Gabby with her wraith research."

"Good," he said, sounding pleased. "Then how did this happen? Would you tell me?"

Taking a deep breath, she explained the comings and goings of the last two weeks, about the curse, the Triskele, what Gabby had found out about the true purpose of the ritual, and everything that had happened since she'd gotten knocked up. Finally, she explained the little she understood about what her little girl was going to become. Guided by light or dark...the immortal witch.

"So it could be any day now," Tristan mused, focusing on the one piece of the puzzle she'd been trying to avoid. The actual birthing part. "Now I understand why Nye was so...protective. I can't imagine him as a father. It took enough convincin' for him to face his feelin's about you."

"I can," she whispered, an image of Nye and his little girl coming to mind. "I have faith. I have to."

Silence stretched between them as they thought over everything they'd confided. Tristan's need to protect his mismatched family had won out over his shame, so he'd returned, and she was glad he had. Hoping some of her faith would rub off on the knight, she took his hand.

After a moment, Isobel asked, "Did you tell Nye the truth? Were you really with Aya?"

Tristan nodded. "She knows me better than I know myself," he explained. "And with her abilities, she was able to look into my mind and see if the compulsion was truly gone. I trust Gabby, I do, but I had to be sure." He glanced away in an attempt to hide the shame flooding his features and let go of her hand. "What I did...it..."

"You don't have to explain yourself," she said when he couldn't continue. "I don't blame you, and neither does Gabby. You needed time to come to terms with it yourself. I understand."

"If I had known Eleanor was renewin' her assault so soon, I would never have left." He glanced at the Triskele pendant hanging around her neck. "I would never..."

"My curse came back," she said, her fingers idly

caressing the jewel. "But it had nothing to do with your compulsion. Nothing at all. Gabby said they were two entirely different spells. A curse can't be removed, like ever. This stops it from progressing." She sighed. "It would've been handy to have the other week, don't you think?"

Tristan smiled. "Now who's focusin' on what ifs?"

Her lips curved upward, and she laughed. "You have a point." Then she got serious, wondering if he'd spoken to the infamous Witch Hunter about their current situation. If anyone knew something, then she had to, right? "Did you happen to ask Aya about the Unhallowed?"

"Yes." He shook his head, and her heart sank. "She didn't know much. To her, wraiths were only a secondhand story. She'd never encountered them, let alone fought one. She tracked dark witches and dealt with them long before it became an issue. I suppose it could be the reason they no longer exist apart from the Unhallowed."

Isobel wasn't comforted. "So after all of this, we still have nothing..."

"Maybe, maybe not," he said in an attempt to reassure her. "She said wraiths were a result of witches turning to dark magic. That delvin' too deep caused some kind of change in their souls. Perhaps it might mean somethin' to Gabby."

"Anyway," she said, attempting to lighten the mood. "She'll be glad to see you when she gets back."

"Gets back?" the knight asked. "Where is she?"

"Shopping for the baby, though I don't think she's coming back with nappies and little pink onesies." Her stomach squirmed, and she winced as she felt the baby plant her foot in for yet another kick. This time, it was higher, signalling she'd flipped and was getting ready to make her grand entrance.

"Are you okay?" the knight asked, reacting to her tensing.

"Yeah, she's just kicking like a ninja. Here..." She grasped the vampire's hands and placed them on her stomach. "Feel that."

The baby kicked again as if she sensed what was happening out in the world, and Tristan's eyes widened.

"I would never do anythin' to harm you, Isobel," he said, glancing at her. "Or the little one. You have to forgive me for leavin'. I—"

"You're a part of this, Tristan," she interrupted him. "You would never knowingly betray us. There is nothing to forgive. *Nothing*."

"Truly?"

"I want you to be here. I want you to be a part of this baby's life. She needs good people around to guide her to the light. She is the most important little girl there'll ever be if you can believe it. Eleanor's coming to take her..." She choked as her throat tightened, a sudden rush of tears threatening to spill. "She's going to try to take her from me."

Tristan glanced at her stomach as the baby kicked again, and something she couldn't quite catch passed over his features.

"I'll be here," he murmured, his brow creasing. "I pledge my life to you and your little one, Isobel. I am yours to command."

Chapter 14

Alex stared down at his sleeping sister and smiled.

When Izzy had told him she was in love with Nye —a vampire—he'd lost the plot. When he'd sacrificed himself over her to become a founder, he'd vowed to protect his family over the generations, using his immortality for good. He'd reacted badly to her and Nye, not because of the fact he was a vampire but because he'd take her future. Children, the whole white picket fence thing. Looking at her now, he wondered if he was more annoyed at himself than at anything the spy could do to put her in jeopardy.

In hindsight, he probably should've been pissed she was hooking up with a vampire more than anything else. He knew exactly what they were capable of. He was still new and had trouble remembering his own strength half the time. Paired with his unbelievable thirst for blood and all the accidental compulsions, he was having a hard time.

But seeing his sister pregnant gave him hope she'd be all right. That they'd have something to fight for after all this was over. Whoever or whatever the little girl turned out to be, he'd be there just as he'd promised.

Isobel began to stir, and her eyes fluttered open. He smiled down at her again, his heart swelling. She'd be a good mom.

"Hey," she said, wiggling into a seated position. "How long have you been there?"

"Not long."

"Sorry, I've been extra sleepy the last day." She rubbed her eyes and scooted off the edge of the bed, her feet hitting the floor.

Gently grasping her arm, Alex helped her to stand. "Are you okay, though? Anything to worry about?"

"If you're asking if the curse is making a comeback, then no. It's the bun in my oven." She smiled and pointed toward the bathroom. "Can you help me? I need to..." She paused, her face beginning to drain of all colour. "Oh..."

"Izzy?"

Her free hand grasped her stomach. "Either I have no bladder control left or my water just broke."

Alex began to panic. "You had better sit back down."

Isobel practically fell back onto the bed and cried

out, her hands clutching the sheets. "Oh, shit," she exclaimed. "*Ohhhhh, shit!*"

"Izzy?" he asked frantically, not knowing what to do.

"Contraction," she hissed through her teeth. "It's gotta be baby time."

"Gabby!" Alex roared, entering full panic mode. He knew nothing about babies, let alone all the *gross* bits. There was always a cut scene in movies and TV shows, so how the hell was he supposed to know what to do?

A moment later, thundering footsteps powered down the hall, and the witch appeared in the doorway.

"What's going on?" she asked, crossing the room. Her eyes widened at the sight of Izzy, and she placed her palm on her forehead, then on her stomach.

"Isobel?" Nye appeared out of thin air, his face looking exactly how Alex felt. Panicked.

"The baby's coming," Gabby confirmed.

"Now?" Nye asked, wringing his hands together.

"It could be hours and hours yet," Gabby replied. "Or considering the pregnancy has been barely nine days, it could be much quicker."

"Great," Alex said, glaring at Nye. "Just what we need on top of everything else. An express lane."

"I've been waiting for the lecture," Nye said, rolling his eyes.

"No lecture," he shot back. "What's done is done."

"I'll say," Isobel declared. "I can't stand to hear your

fighting, not when I'm about to shove a baby out of my vagina."

"Whoa!" Alex exclaimed, covering his eyes. "Too much information!"

She slapped him on the arm. "Smartass." Then her smile faded as another contraction came.

Alex glanced around the room, his smile fading when he saw the matching looks on Nye and Gabby's faces. They were worried.

"Guys?" he asked softly, not wanting to alarm his sister.

Gabby nodded once, and Nye rounded the bed, taking the free side by Isobel. Somehow, Eleanor would know when the baby was coming and would make a kidnapping attempt. What was it that the witch had explained to him? To turn to the light and shape her future, the baby had to bond with her parents— her *real* parents.

"She's coming, isn't she?" Isobel asked, not missing a beat. "She's coming to take my baby before I can even see her. She's going to take her and use her as a...*thing*."

"We won't let her," Nye said, clutching her hand. "We'll stop her before she even lays eyes on you. I'll tear her apart with my bare hands if I have to. She will not get into this house."

"Stay here with her," Gabby said to the spy. "We'll handle Eleanor."

"You're leaving me?" Isobel exclaimed, crying out as another contraction tore through her stomach.

"You'll be fine with Nye," the witch replied. "You have to be. Magic needs to fight magic."

"But—"

"You'll be fine," Alex interrupted her. "If anything happens—*which it won't*—he'll be able to heal you."

"Tell Tristan to call the Six," Nye barked. "Get as many hands here as they can. We'll need everything we've got to fend her off." Turning to Isobel, he placed a kiss on her forehead. "I'll be a minute, love. I'll be right back, and then we'll do this together."

She nodded, the labor already beginning to take its toll on her body. It was going to happen fast, and he hoped Nye had the guts to stand by her until the end.

The group filtered out of the room, leaving her in peace, and Alex lingered, making sure his sister was settled before he joined the others.

"Alex," Isobel said, grasping his hand. "If they fight her off this time...what happens when she comes back? Eleanor won't stop until she has what she wants." Her hands curled into the sheets as yet another contraction twisted her stomach.

"Then we'll fight her again," he replied. "And again and again until we find a way to get rid of her for good."

"I'm sorry," she said, her brow spotted with sweat. "I never meant for things to—"

"Don't even say it, Iz. No regrets, okay?"

She nodded and moaned, screwing her eyes shut.

"You know what sucks about giving birth to a magical baby?"

"What?"

"No hospital. That's where they keep the painkillers, you know."

Gabby stood on the back patio, the last rays of sunlight fading over the horizon.

All was quiet apart from the normal sounds of the city. Cars *whooshed* by on the street outside, a dog barked a few houses down, a door slammed, music filtered up the hill from the heath. Human life was going on even as a magical battle was about to be waged. Thankfully, none of them would hear a thing that happened within the manor grounds. She'd seen to that.

Glancing over the assembled army of vampires, she studied each one, grimacing at some of the hardened faces. Nye really knew some thuggish vampires, having made the best of the bunch for the new incarnation of the Six. They were loyal to the spy, and in turn, they were loyal to her. Thankfully, the presence of Isobel and the baby were kept secret, and they believed they were fighting for the well-being of the London vampires—which was true. A few omissions had been made for the good of everyone.

She saw Reed standing with Tristan—father and

son—and she raised her eyebrows at the younger vampire. He caught her gaze and shook his head. He hadn't told him yet, and now wasn't really the time for a family reunion, but she could see the hope hovering around him.

When she'd heard the knight had returned, she'd been relieved, to say the least. Then Isobel had explained he'd offered his life to Nye—who'd almost taken it—but had reconsidered at the last minute. Vampires criticised witches for their weird and wonderful ways, but theirs? Man, they were crazy.

"We form a tight web around Eleanor," Tristan was saying. "When she appears, we force her back. Gabby will use her power to shield us as best as she can."

"How are we meant to fight a wraith?" one of the vampires asked. "I thought you killed them all already."

"One slipped away," Gabby said, voicing the suspicions she'd had all this time. That the night of the ritual, she'd almost overwhelmed them to the point she could have let them slip into oblivion, but the others had sacrificed their power so that Eleanor could go on.

The theory she'd been mulling over since Isobel's pregnancy had come to light was to drain the wraith's battery to zero, and only then would the Unhallowed be truly gone from the land of the living. But a theory wasn't solid, and they couldn't bank on it, not yet. Besides, Gabby didn't have enough power to face a fully powered-up wraith and win. Her other theory was to do with the baby, and she didn't like it at all. No, that theory would make her become exactly like Eleanor despite all the good intentions in the world.

"We're here to buy time," Tristan said. "Protect and repel. Nothin' more. Gabby will do what she can. Those are Nye's orders."

"Where is Nye?" another vampire said. "Why isn't he here fighting? Regulus would have stood with us."

"Nye is protecting something far more precious than your sorry ass," Alex said. "You want a founder to back you up when you piss your pants? Well, you got one."

Gabby snorted at the irony. Alex defending Nye? Miracles did happen.

The vampire standing next to the founder balked. "You're…"

He scowled at the man, who was at least three times the size of him. "The one and only."

Alex had come a long way from the days of his nerdy, gangly youth, that was for sure.

The air began to ping with an electrical charge, and Gabby straightened up, pointing to the far end of the yard. "The wards have sounded," she cried. "Look alive, she's here."

A dark mist began to pool at the far corner of the grounds, the small sliver of moon hardly lighting much at all. The longer Gabby stared at it, the more she realised it was pulling everything into it like a black hole. Not even the bright lights of the manor could penetrate the growing darkness.

Her heart grew heavy as she realised what she'd faced at the ritual was nothing compared to the power Eleanor had gathered since. This might be the end of the line.

A human form materialised through the vapour, and the wraith appeared. Eleanor stood at the bottom of the garden, a sole figure among the greenery. Her hair was loose, her wild curls fluttering in the breeze, and her waifish form made her seem weaker than she was. This tiny, sweet-looking woman was much more than she seemed on the surface. None of them could underestimate her if they wanted to get out of this alive.

Gabby peered at her, squinting as Eleanor's form flickered slightly, shimmering from solid into the mass of cloud and lightning she'd seen the night of the ritual. Her wraith form was coming out to play, being held just below the surface ready to strike like a snake.

"You have something of mine," she said, staring straight at Gabby. "I've come to collect."

"Over my dead body, bitch," she spat, reaching for the coil of darkness at the base of her soul.

Gabby had used the untapped power inside of her once to send the wraiths back to the brink, and she would use it again. She was strong now, and the lure of ultimate power wouldn't take her. She'd come back.

"That can be arranged," the wraith said with a smirk. "Quite easily."

Raising her hand, Eleanor called on her magic, the air beginning to charge with static. The vampires around her tensed, their fangs bared, ready to strike.

Gabby raised her own hand, mirroring Eleanor's stance, calling upon her own abilities. Time to show that bitch who was the boss. The good guys were going to kick her ass back to the other side and beyond.

The wraith smiled, her eyes sparkling, then she flung her hands toward the assembled vampires, an invisible wall smashing into their bodies, sending them all flying backward. When they tried to stand and counter attack, none of them could move, the spell holding them in place.

Eleanor began to laugh and walked across the lawn toward Gabby. "Nice trick, no?"

"You think you have all the power here," Gabby snarled. "Do you know what'll be your downfall?"

The wraith tilted her head to the side, her curled hair waving in the breeze of the witch's brewing power.

"*Arrogance.*"

Gabby cried out, bringing her own power back against the wall, and the spell crumbled, freeing the vampires from the force pinning them down.

Immediately, they sprang to their feet and leapt into action, Alex, Tristan, and Reed among them. Vampires piled on top of the wraith, and she began to writhe under the mountain of flesh, the scent of blood tickling Gabby's nose. It couldn't be that easy, right?

A bright light began to grow from within, and Gabby knew it was only the beginning. The real fight hadn't even started. A sharp burst of energy sent the vampires flying once more, Eleanor emerging unscathed, a look of pure malice etched on her face.

Then all hell broke loose.

***

Nye returned to Isobel as fast as he could.

He busied himself laying out towels on the bed, placing pillows behind Isobel's back, dabbing her forehead with a cool washcloth, anything to make her more comfortable. The longer he watched, the more hopeless he felt. He could do nothing to alleviate her pain. He had four hundred years of knowledge and understanding but when it came to this? He was at a complete and total loss.

Her contractions were closer and closer, his nerves shredding along with each bout of pain she endured.

"You look sick," Isobel said as she breathed through the spasms.

"I'm fine," he replied. "Just worried about you."

"I want to push," she said abruptly, her voice wavering. "I feel like I want to squeeze her out. You need to check."

He glanced at her stomach and the sheet that covered her and swallowed.

"Nye," she snapped. "It's the last thing I want you to be doing too, you know. It's gross and totally unsexy, but you have to help her out."

He hesitated, a million and one terrible scenarios going through his mind. What if the baby got caught? What if the umbilical cord was wrapped around her neck? What if she didn't start breathing on her own? What if Isobel haemorrhaged? Would he have enough wits about him to help her before she bled out?

"*Ooohhhh!*" Isobel cried. "She's coming!"

Swallowing his fear, he got into position. Someone had to catch the little one, so it may as well be her dad.

Ready or not...

<hr>

The wind dropped suddenly, sending the vampires tumbling to the ground, each of them unconscious.

Eleanor turned on her heel and stared up at the house, her lips curving into a satisfied smirk.

Gabby stilled, her heart thudding in her chest, and she knew. The baby had been born.

Eleanor pushed against her with a barrage of force, her essence seeming to draw power from everything around her. She was sucking the life from the garden, the plants beginning to wilt and the leaves fading from green to yellow to orange before fluttering to the ground. The wraith was far stronger than Gabby had thought, siphoning power recklessly from the earth Gabby had sworn to protect.

Gabby struggled to hold her position, begging for enough time for the baby to bond with her parents so the light would take her instead of the darkness. Everything depended on it. *Everything.*

Sensing her faltering strength, Eleanor pushed with everything she could muster and Gabby's magic crumbled, shattering into nothing.

Her head cracked on the flagstones, her head spinning. Eleanor stood over her, smiling in triumph as her vision slipped...

Then everything went back.

"Oh, God," Nye exclaimed as he watched his daughter come into the world. "*Oh, God.*"

Isobel grunted, giving one last push, and the baby slid out into his hands.

"Bloody hell!" he said, cradling the little mess of arms and legs in his arms. His shirt was ruined.

"Is she..." Isobel gasped, completely breathless.

His stomach rolled as he cut the umbilical cord and wiped the gunk off her skin with a soft towel. Rubbing her back, her chest began to rise, her lungs filling with her first breath.

"She's okay," he murmured, starting to tear up. "You're okay. Everything is fine. Just fine."

The baby opened her eyes then, revealing two bright little irises, and she stared at him. Something passed between them—a zap of energy, a bolt of love, a profound sense of...something. He didn't know what it was, but he knew the little girl was everything they thought she'd be. She was a very special witch. He could feel it all around her.

"Quick," Isobel said, her breathing laboured. "Ismena's tear." She held out her hand and waved at the box on the bedside table.

Nye snatched it up and opened the lid, staring at the little jewel. Outside, the wind had died down, the crashing and banging falling into silence. Eleanor was coming.

Nye slipped the tear around the baby's neck, her little arms flailing as her first cries echoed around the room.

"Here," Nye said, transferring the little bundle into Isobel's arms so she could feel the same connection he had. "Protect her. I've got you both."

Movement at the door drew his attention, and he rose to his feet, baring his fangs.

Eleanor stepped inside, her expression melting when she saw the child. "Oh! She's beautiful," she crooned. "She'll be a fine addition to the coven. A very fine addition indeed."

"Like hell," Nye snarled as he shot forward, aiming for her throat.

Before he could even take a second step, the wraith flung her hand at him, and his body flew across the room, his back slamming into the wall. He felt her evil web clinging to his limbs and knew it was no use. He was stuck.

"No!" Isobel cried, causing the baby to stir.

Eleanor crossed the room, a sweet smile on her face. To think he'd once believed he loved a poisonous woman like her! It made him sick to see her twisted into this dark creature, hell-bent on stealing a child—his child—that he'd only held for the smallest fraction of time. It was abhorrent.

Nye writhed, using all of his strength in an attempt to break free of Eleanor's hold, but it was no use. He was fixed in place, helpless as the wraith stood over Isobel and the baby. *No!*

As Eleanor stared at the child, the strangest thing happened. Her eyes widened in fear. *Fear.*

"No, no, no..." she muttered.

"Get away from her, you monster," Isobel hissed.

Nye struggled, his heart breaking. She was powerless lying there, she had no power, no strength, and the child was completely defenceless...but something had Eleanor recoiling in shock.

The tear. It had to be!

"You can't take her from me," Isobel cried, tears streaming down her face as she clutched the baby to her chest. "They protect her now. She'll never be taken by your poisonous darkness."

Nye's gaze flew to the tear he'd placed around the baby's neck and gritted his teeth together. The little jewel was beginning to glow brighter and brighter until he had to squint. The baby began to cry, its shrill little voice the only sound he could hear. Then as fast as it had grown, the light subsided, revealing the room once more.

Nye fell, the spell holding him prisoner dissolving, and he fell face first onto the floor with a thud. When he managed to scramble to his feet, Eleanor was gone.

Darting to the bed, he let out a relieved sigh when he found Isobel cradling the baby, both of them safe and sound.

They'd done it.

Chapter 15

Gabby stood in the middle of the lawn, staring at the mess Eleanor had left behind.

The beautiful garden that'd been bursting with luscious green trees and hundreds of flowers in full bloom was nothing but a decaying mess. Everything was brown and wilted, and the summer sun had caused the garden beds to emit a stench that was pungent to even her nose.

She glanced over at Regulus's olive tree. It stood as tall and proud as ever, its branches full of bright green leaves. Ironic that it was the only plant unaffected by the chaos that had ripped through the place the night before last, but the magic that protected it was a web of her own creation. It was flawless. Of course, it was.

Tristan stood beside her, stoic as ever except for the slight wrinkle in his forehead. He was having trouble tolerating the stink, too.

"Gross, right?" she said, scowling at the mess.

"This will take weeks to clean up," he said in commiseration. "We'll have to get a landscaper to come in as soon as possible. Compel them to not ask questions."

Her scowl deepened. "No need. It's my mess. I'll fix it."

"Is your head hurtin'? If so, we can take a break. The wards are stronger than ever."

She ignored him, wondering how much power it would take to grow back the entire garden. The lawn, trees, flowers, the pot plants, the Virginia creeper she loved so much. Well, *everything*.

"Gabby, if you'll just let me—"

"No," she snapped. "I'm fine. It's just a bump."

"I know you blame yourself for lettin' Eleanor get so close to Isobel, but—"

"Tristan, *please*." She shot him a warning glance.

"They're fine," he said firmly. "Everyone is fine. No one was hurt badly."

"Are *you* fine?"

"I saw them a few minutes ago," he went on, ignoring her on purpose. "Isobel is walkin' the baby around the kitchen tryin' to get her to fall asleep. I told her she should rest herself, but she seems unnaturally energised."

Gabby grunted. "Nothing about any of this is natural."

"No, I suppose not. The baby has already opened

her eyes," he mused. "She has an awareness that's unnervin' for such a little creature."

Gabby gritted her teeth, doing her darnedest to hold onto her emotions. She felt a burning sensation in the back of her throat at the thought she let Eleanor pass. The wraith had stood over her friend's bed while Nye had been rendered helpless—the baby cradled in her mother's arms—and had almost snatched her child away. If it weren't for Ismena's tear, then today would be a much different day.

Gabby swallowed the regret at her failure and brought herself back under control. She was just tired from the struggle against Eleanor and the effort it had taken to reinstate the wards that morning. She was so beat that Tristan had to accompany her and lend his strength so the job could get done.

"Why do you stay?" he asked abruptly. "There are so many bad memories in this place."

"Why did you come back when you did?" she asked, turning his questioning on him.

Tristan's expression didn't budge an inch.

"Arrow made me see I was merely runnin' away from my problems, not facin' them," he said as if it were the most simple thing in the world. "I came back to atone."

"Atone for what? Compulsion is a normal part of a vampire's life."

His lips quirked. "Hypocritical of me, no?"

"I didn't mean it like that." Her shoulders sank, and she felt a pang of regret at her hasty words.

"No one is one hundred percent good, I suppose," he replied, turning his attention back to the green. "We all have things to atone for in one way or another. Things we regret and actions we wish to right."

Thinking of the dark power coiled at the very bottom of her soul, Gabby grimaced. The things she'd done to save her friends could fall into the column labeled good or the one labeled bad. Did she have to atone for her actions? Both sides lived within her, but then again, life was about balancing the two halves of herself just as any human, witch, or vampire.

Which was exactly the fight Isobel and Nye's daughter would have to face.

Thinking about her own desire for a family—out of want, not duty as a witch—she mulled over the baby and what they would have to do next. The only way to stop Eleanor resurrecting the Unhallowed was to protect the still unnamed baby...and the only way to destroy them forever was to exploit the child's power in the exact same fashion the wraith was going to. The thought made Gabby sick and entirely hypocritical.

In witch lore, there was always another way, but perhaps this time, there wasn't.

"Come inside," Tristan said, breaking her chaotic thought pattern. "The garden can wait."

She glanced over her shoulder and caught sight of

Reed talking with Alex by the entrance to the opposite wing of the house. Talking about family…

Turning back to the knight, she said, "I need some time to think. I'll be in shortly."

He nodded slightly, like he was acknowledging a noble lady of yore, and retreated across the wilted lawn.

Perhaps Gabby would find her future a little closer to home than she realised.

———

Isobel cradled her daughter in her arms and bounced her gently, attempting to rock her to sleep. Needless to say, the way she was staring up at her right now, it wasn't doing any good.

Rounding the kitchen island on her tenth rotation, she caught another glimpse of the withered garden. Most of the greenery had decayed, and it was a confronting sight.

Only a day had passed since Eleanor's assault on the manor, and everyone and everything was still in disarray, though the cleanup was starting to progress. Nye had sent the Six out to scour the city for any clues as to where Eleanor crawled away to and to gather intelligence on the vampires and what they did and did not know. Tristan was assisting Gabby around the grounds, lending her his strength to reinstate the wards. And Alex had gone to the store to get the much-needed baby supplies.

Isobel knew she shouldn't be on her feet, especially since it had only been a day since she'd given birth. The fears her body would crumble the moment she was no longer needed to incubate the child were unfounded. Maybe she should be alarmed, but deep down, she was relieved. Unfortunately, the feeling fine part didn't apply to her post-baby stomach flab.

Isobel stared out the window and watched the goings-on. Gabby stood in the middle of the pile of dirt that used to be the lawn, her back to the manor. The witch blamed herself for letting Eleanor get so close to them, but there was nothing she could have done. The bump on her head that she'd received when she fell onto the patio was still present on her temple, and she refused to let any of the vampires heal her.

Everyone was fine. The vampires, Tristan, Reed, Nye, Isobel, and the baby. Ismena's tear had protected them in the end, and to Isobel, it was enough. Her friend put too much pressure on herself.

The baby squirmed in her arms, her little mouth opening with a wide yawn. Her brown eyes stared up at her, and Isobel smiled, wondering how such a little thing could hold her heart so tightly.

Considering the amount of time that had passed since she'd come into the world, Isobel was amazed at the things her daughter was doing. She'd expected the child to be gifted but from day dot? It was something else. She hardly slept, she was always hungry—which meant there'd been a lot of diaper emergencies already—but she didn't cry at all. There were a few grumbles and a fat tear or two, but no full-blown screaming. She was a dream baby if anyone asked Isobel. Total smooth sailing.

The baby gurgled in her arms, and Isobel glanced down, smiling at the sight of her little face. The shock of bright orange hair under her little white beanie was a surprise when Isobel first realised she was going to take after her mom, but it was growing on her. Her little ginger ninja.

"Hey, baby," she crooned. "Shall we go see what your daddy is up to? He's been hiding out this morning, doing who knows what. Heaven help me if you've inherited any of his cunningness."

The baby squirmed again, wanting to free her arms from the cocoon that was her blanket. Loosening the fabric, Isobel tilted her face out of the way as her daughter's little arms flailed happily.

"I'll take that as a yes," she declared and wove her way through the house and back upstairs.

Nye wasn't in the study as he usually was, so she moved down the hall to their room. Peering in the door, she saw him securing a screw into a piece of flat-pack furniture, the Allen key looking totally alien in his hands. Her vampire boyfriend putting together a flat-pack her vampire brother brought back from Ikea? If only she had a camera!

He was surrounded by discarded cardboard, Styrofoam, and plastic, an assembled cot standing in the centre of the chaos. Eyeballs deep in another kind of trouble, then.

"What's this?" she asked, stepping into the room.

Nye glanced up and smiled. "Alex brought it back this morning," he said. "She's got to sleep someplace."

"We've got to stop calling her she," she muttered, rocking the baby back and forth. "Any ideas?"

Nye stood before her, only having eyes for the little bundle in her arms. "She's going to grow up to be an immortal witch, so it has to be something badass."

Isobel raised an eyebrow, stifling a laugh. "Let me just Google 'badass baby names' and see what we come up with."

He sniggered and retrieved the mattress, placing it into the finished cot Then he arranged the sheets and blankets, gesturing for the baby. Taking her gently from Isobel's arms, he set her into his masterpiece, tucking the blanket around her little body. Immediately, her arms flailed, and her hand wrapped around one of his fingers.

"As I live and breathe," he whispered. "What a smart little girl you are."

Seeing the battle-toughened vampire so enamoured with a day-and-a-half-old baby made Isobel melt even more. She always thought he was handsome, but right now, he was irresistible.

"She's growing. Do you see it?" he asked, glancing at her.

Bending over the cot, Isobel studied her daughter but didn't really know what a baby this small was meant to look like, let alone be able to do.

"I don't know," she said. "I've not got much experience with babies."

"She's..." He frowned, wiggling the finger the baby still held onto.

Thinking about the moment she'd held her daughter in her arms for the first time, Isobel remembered the odd sensation that'd overcome her when their gazes had met. Which was strange enough considering the baby shouldn't have been able to open her eyes right away.

"Did you feel it, too?" she asked. "When I held her for the first time, she looked right at me, Nye. She was minutes old, and *she looked at me*."

He nodded, extracting his hand from the cot and fixing the blankets in place. "I think that was the bond Gabby was talking about. She's going to be okay, Isobel."

"I hope so."

They watched their daughter for a moment, marvelling at the unexpected thing they'd created.

"Any ideas on a name?" Nye asked.

"Ismena," she replied, smoothing her fingertip against the little girl's cheek. "I think we should name her after the witch who saved her."

"Ismena," Nye echoed. "Two Izzys."

She smiled at the similarities in their names. "Then Ismena it is." The baby flailed her arms wildly, and Isobel leaned over to fix the blankets once more. "Do you like that? Little Ismena. That's what we'll call you."

When she was done, she glanced up at Nye, and her smile faded. He looked positively forlorn.

"Are you okay?"

"Me?" he asked. "Of course."

"Don't lie to me, Nye," she said haughtily. "I know when you're using your dismissive king of the London underworld technique on me."

"Dammit," he cursed.

"And you wouldn't dare use compulsion to avoid talking."

"That'd be selfish," he said, feigning horror at the suggestion.

"That'd be a death wish."

They stared at one another, and when Isobel could take it no more, she burst out laughing. Nye smirked, then glanced back to Ismena.

"Being a father never crossed my mind," he declared, his voice taking on a more serious tone.

"What, never?" she asked. "Not even when you were human?"

He shook his head, his expression changing. "It was never possible. Before or after. It just was just a fact, so I stopped thinking about it. As a spy, love was a liability, so a child would have been another tool to use against me. As a vampire, death took my humanity and my ability to procreate." He sighed. "Perhaps deep down, I wanted all those things, so that was why I took an interest in the little girl in the Tower."

"What little girl?" Isobel frowned, not knowing the exact story of how Nye had become a vampire. She'd quizzed him mercilessly about life in the golden era of England under the rule of Queen Elizabeth I for her thesis, but he'd never mentioned a little girl before.

"After the Spanish Armada attacked England in 1588 and my face was ruined in the battle, I wasn't able to go back to my work as a spy. I was disfigured, and it made me easily recognisable." He gestured to the scar that ran through his left eyebrow, across the bridge of his nose, and finished on his opposite cheek. Isobel hardly noticed it anymore, let alone thought it marred his features. To her, he was handsome all the same.

"I was forced to work closer to home in London," he went on. "A slew of murders drew the attention of the guard, and after an investigation, a girl was caught in the act. She was imprisoned in the bottommost reaches of the Tower."

"How old was she?"

"Young. Around ten or so. I can scarcely remember."

"Ten years old?" Isobel exclaimed.

"They threw her into a putrid cell and forgot she existed, all because no one knew what to do with her. She wouldn't talk, and she'd fight anyone who neared.

She was completely feral. I wanted to win her trust and find the truth. I'd solve what no one else could and prove my worth." He turned away from the cot as if his words might affect Ismena. "I cared for her when no one else would. I sat with her and told her stories. I brought her food that went untouched. I gave her a doll and carved her a little spinning top she could play with. Anything to gain her trust. Eventually, she started giving in, and before long, she told me anything I wanted to know. Except, I didn't know the right questions to ask..."

"You saw her as a daughter?" Isobel asked gently.

"I cared for her, yes," he replied. "As a daughter? Who knows, but I didn't realise she was a vampire. They were as mystical to me then as they were to you before we met. She must have compelled me because the next thing I knew, I was inside the cell with her. Her defining moment as a human child was her longing for her mother and father. I suppose she saw my kindness and latched onto me. I don't remember how I died, just how I came back. When a guard finally came looking for me, blood was the only thing I wanted."

Isobel didn't know what to say. Nye had cared for an unwanted little girl, a child who he thought was incapable of the murders she was accused of, only to find she was a vampire. His caring for her had caused him to turn against his will.

"That's why children should never be turned. Why

they should never be used. I couldn't chance her changing someone else," he went on. "I... A little girl..."

"She wasn't a child anymore," she said firmly, understanding how his past had shaped his future fears. "Ismena isn't going to turn out the same as that girl."

"Did you want to have a family?" he asked, signalling he was finished talking about that time in his life.

"You know what I wanted," Isobel replied. "A family was an option but not right away. I had things I wanted to do."

"You're likely the only person I know who was certain of the life she wanted to live," he said morosely.

"Plans change," she retorted. "Life is unpredictable."

"I was so certain of who I was," he said, staring down at his daughter. "Then Zac and Aya blew through everything, the Six fell apart, and Regulus died fighting Aed. I never wanted to be the leader of the London vampires, but everyone wanted me to do it. I was the logical choice. Whatever they saw in me, I wanted to see it, too. I know that now."

Isobel pressed her arm against his. "And now? Do you see it?"

He shrugged. "I don't even know what 'it' is."

She sensed his uncertainty and leaned into him,

relishing the closeness that had become easier for him to tolerate in the wake of Ismena's birth.

"Do you want to be the leader of the London vampires?"

"I don't know," he replied. "After the Six... I was lost. After hundreds of years knowing who I was, I wasn't so sure anymore. Doing this...it gave me something to define myself with."

"Having power could protect her, you know."

"It would." He grunted and shook his head. "We'll work it out, sooner or later."

Isobel's mouth dropped open. "We? You and me? You'd ask me what I wanted? That's a shocker coming from the guy who kidnapped me for my 'own protection.'" She air quoted the last part.

With a deadpan expression, he said, "Of course. I was never going to be able to rule like Regulus did. He was untouchable to everyone and everything, even love. At least, he was until Gabby came along. Besides, I'm not Regulus. That's especially clear now Ismena is here. She needs a happy home. If that means I have to rule a different way or take business elsewhere where she's not a part of it, then I'll do whatever's necessary."

Whatever's necessary... Nye's words echoed through her mind, and she began to understand what being a parent was all about. Doing whatever it took to ensure the well-being of her child. It was especially clear given the chaos that was their lives. Supernatural revenge plots, crazy fertility rituals, wraiths, spirits, magical tears... What a world little Ismena had been born into.

"I worry for her," Isobel murmured, watching Ismena's eyes droop until they finally closed. "She's going to have a hard life, no matter what we do to help her."

"I know," Nye said, placing his hand on her back. "There's not much we can do except be here. Gabby will teach her to control her powers, and she'll have an immortal uncle to look out for her when she grows up."

"What about you?" she asked, glancing at him. "You're immortal."

He shrugged. "It's not a permanent fixture for me, not like for Alex. I can be taken away at any moment, but your brother can only be taken by one person— Aya—and I doubt she would end him anytime soon. At least, not without express permission."

Isobel felt an overwhelming need to cry at that moment. She was mortal, and her daughter was going to live forever.

"Isobel?"

She shook her head, her eyes misting with tears.

"What's wrong?" Nye asked, rubbing her back.

"She's going to live forever, and I'm not going to be here for her." She hiccupped and turned into him, burying her face into the crook of his neck.

"We're going to be okay," he crooned. "This story has a different ending. It has to."

Chapter 16

I sobel stood on the balcony overlooking the back garden and watched Ismena run around in circles on the wilted lawn while Gabby attempted to catch her.

That's right. Ismena was *running*.

It only felt like the day before that her daughter was lying in the tiny cot her father had built for her, barely the size of a watermelon. Isobel sighed, wondering how she managed to keep her daughter alive at all considering she was comparing her to fruit.

Two weeks had passed since Ismena was born, and in those scant few days, she'd grown faster than anyone had anticipated. She'd said her first word when she was a week old, gurgling *Mom* and *Dad*, her flame-red hair had reached the middle of her back, her features had defined into the spitting image of Nye's, and her power had manifested the moment she'd been able to stand up.

She was growing so fast it was hard to keep her clothed at all. Outfits came in, and then a day later, they were folded away in a case ready to be donated to goodwill in as new condition. Her appetite never slowed, and at every meal, she would inhale everything on her plate and still look for more. She needed something to fuel her accelerated growth spurt, after all.

They didn't know if her life was limited or if she'd grow to maturity and remain immortal, or if she'd die once her destiny was fulfilled. Whatever her destiny was now that they'd managed to keep her with them and focused on the light, they didn't know.

Everyone had become attached to Ismena quickly, especially her and Nye. Whatever happened, she didn't want to believe her daughter was nothing more than a tool for the Unhallowed's resurrection. She had a life now—a free life—and there was more out there for her than being a psychopathic wraith's battery pack.

Isobel glanced up as Nye appeared beside her, seeming to have finished organising his diabolical vampire empire for the day.

"What are you looking at?" he asked before placing a chaste kiss on her temple.

"She's two weeks old," she said, pointing to the garden. "Look at her."

Nye narrowed his eyes at the witches on the lawn, and whatever he was thinking he kept to himself.

"She's growing faster than she ever did in my stomach," Isobel went on. "And don't get me started on her powers. She had a tantrum and made my coffee mug explode yesterday."

"She was always going to be more than normal," Nye said. "Don't tell me the thought of her growing up fast never crossed your mind because I'm pretty sure we all had it at some point."

"I was too busy rolling around the house," she retorted. "Or do you have the memory of a goldfish?"

Nye snorted, hiding a laugh, and she slapped him on the arm.

"Look at her, Isobel," he said, nodding at Ismena, who was chattering away happily with Gabby. "She's happy. She's healthy. She's already learning how to control her powers. So none of this is normal, but what's normal when I'm a vampire, Gabby's a witch, and you're the mother of a magical baby with a two-week gestation period? She'll be okay."

Isobel nodded, not able to voice her real fear. That Eleanor would come back and take Ismena from them. Their first duty was to their daughter, but what if they still couldn't fight the Unhallowed and win? What if they were forced to use their sweet, little girl the same way Eleanor was going to? She was just an innocent child.

"There you are," came the sound of Alex's voice behind them.

Turning, Isobel saw the pile of shopping bags clutched in his hands and shook her head. Despite her fears, Ismena had the most mismatched family around to keep her safe. It was one beacon in the uncertainty of their immediate future.

"Alex, you didn't," she said with a groan.

"What?" he asked with a mischievous grin. "Can't I buy my niece a giant pile of toys?"

"She'll grow out of them in a few weeks," Nye grumbled. "Then what'll you do with them?"

"So what? She's still a kid now. She should have something to play with other than her grumpy father."

Isobel plucked some of the bags out of her brother's hand and began sifting through them. There was a selection of My Little Ponies, Barbie dolls, and soft toys. She held up a bright yellow container filled with building blocks and was certain Ismena was a pretty lucky girl to have an immortal uncle with deep pockets.

"He has a point, Nye," she said, putting the toys back into the bags. "Mena is still a little girl, no matter how fast she's growing up. We should let her be one while she has the chance."

"Is she, though? A little girl?" the spy asked. "She's the Immortal Witch."

"Infinite knowledge and understanding," she mused. "I'm pretty sure that's how Gabby described it."

"Infinite *whatever*," Alex declared. "No matter what she's meant to be or do, she still needs to have fun."

"Go give them to her already," Isobel declared, waving him off. "And while you're at it, take the..." Her words trailed off with a groan as Alex bounded over the balcony, hopped onto the roof, and landed on the lawn below. "...stairs."

"He won't listen to you," Nye said. "He's smitten."

"I suppose that means you can keep your head?"

He smirked. "For now."

Turning to watch the goings-on in the garden, she laughed as Ismena began pulling at the bags in her uncle's hands. He lifted them up out of reach, but she jumped...and *floated* for a split second before returning lithely to the ground. The things she could do already were astounding. Soon, she'd leave her poor mother behind.

"Come," Nye said as Alex led their daughter inside so she could open her presents. "Let's oversee the mess that's about to explode all over the house."

It was moments like these she'd cherish when Ismena was grown, and knowing how soon that would be, Isobel's heart sank. How big would she be when her first Christmas came around? Twenty-one?

Shaking her head, she followed Nye into the house, determined not to think about it.

Tristan listened to the sounds of glee coming from the living room at the front of the house and tried to find happiness in Ismena's joy, but he couldn't find it within himself. Alex had purchased more toys than was likely appropriate, but the little witch sounded more than pleased.

Sitting at the island bench in the kitchen, he stared out over the wilted garden and sighed.

On the outside, he might look like a thirty-year-old man, but on the inside, he was worn down by the ages, his continued struggle with his past and loyalties a constant drag on his day-to-day life. Gabby had removed Eleanor's compulsion, and his visit with Arrow had confirmed it, but he still didn't feel right about any of it.

He should've been able to withstand the wraith's power and break free. The problem was, he hadn't known he was under her control until he was standing over Gabby at the standing stones, entirely prepared to rip her apart...just like he'd torn Nye's witch contact, Sabine, limb from limb.

Resting his head in his palms, he tried to clear his mind of the image but wasn't having much luck. He'd done terrible things over the millennia, especially in the first decade of his vampire life. He'd slaughtered innocents who'd strayed too close to his hideaway in the forest of Germany. He'd killed so many that the local peasants had referred to him as the 'Devil Who

Walked.' His legacy of murder was so strong they still told stories about the monster who lurked in the woods to this day.

He wasn't that person anymore, not after Arrow helped him control what he'd become and remember his humanity, but the compulsion Eleanor had placed him under brought back all those memories. The sense his life was not in his own hands, that he'd killed innocents, that he almost killed Gabby...the thought was too much to bear for a man like him. A knight who believed in loyalty and a strict code of honour above all else.

Movement roused him from his self-loathing, and he raised his head. Ismena was standing beside him, her little hand tugging at the hem of his shirt.

"Hello, little one," he said, surprised to see her wandering the house on her own. "Where has everyone gone?"

Ismena was already grown enough to play quietly and not need constant vigilance, but Isobel hadn't let her out of her sight since she was born.

She smiled up at him expectantly, like she knew he was worried about something and was waiting for him to tell her.

"Do you need somethin'?" he asked. "Are you hungry?"

She shook her head and tugged on his shirt once more a frown pulling at her mouth.

Tristan shoved off the chair and knelt before the little girl, who only stood there and watched him with her strange honey coloured eyes. Even he could see there was a depth in her that shouldn't be present in a two-year-old child, and it was unnerving. How much did she understand and was unable to voice? Perhaps she did sense his melancholy and desired to help.

"I don't know how much you can understand," he said, smoothing back her fire-like hair. "But I need to tell someone, and perhaps you are the perfect little princess who could listen."

She stared up at him expectantly, her honey eyes sparkling with curiosity. What a strange little creature she was. He'd never had much interaction with children after he turned, but little Ismena stirred memories of his own daughter. When his human life had been taken from him, it'd been years since he'd seen his family. The Crusades had been brutal, and many men had been parted from families the same as his. He never knew what became of his wife and daughter, but he hoped they'd found happiness after his loss.

"I can't trust myself," he said, his thoughts heavy with the absence of his family. "Eleanor cast her compulsion on me, and I feel as if I might turn at any moment. What if I'm not safe? What if I hurt you without knowing what I'm doin'?" He cast his gaze to the floor and shook his head. "I don't belong anymore. I lost my family a very long time ago. I can't be the cause of this one's demise."

He glanced up in surprise as a little hand brushed against his cheek, and her warm skin began to heat his coldness.

"Happy!" she chortled, then grasped his hand, tugging him forward.

He blinked, his throat feeling tight with emotion. With one word, she'd dismissed a thousand years of anguish, and he felt lighter. Had she placed some of her power inside him?

"Where are we goin'?" he asked as he rose, and she led him through the house, her tiny feet treading purposely as they went.

She didn't reply, determined in her course. When they entered the living room at the front of the manor, she saw the mess of toys and smiled.

Immediately, Ismena threw herself down onto the floor and upended the plastic container, spilling coloured blocks over the floor.

"Block!" she cried, looking up at him with sparkling eyes, a wide smile on her face.

"Do you wish me to play?" he asked, sitting cross-legged on the floor.

Clapping her hands, the blocks began to rise up off the floor, hovering in the air.

"That's quite impressive," he said, plucking up a green rectangle. "Can you build a tower?"

She nodded and squinted her eyes. Immediately, he felt the air tingle with power, and the blocks began to float, merging with one another. First, the foundation formed and then the walls, each little piece of plastic clicking into place until there were no more that fit.

When she was done, Ismena smiled up at Tristan, extremely pleased with her handiwork. Then she clapped her hands once more, and the entire thing crumbled to the ground.

If this was her level of control after two weeks, even at her accelerated growth, then she was going to be a very powerful witch, indeed. In all his years hunting dark witches with Arrow, he'd never seen a child display such talents. A child who manifested power other than an accidental burst of psychic ability was a rare occurrence. Ismena was incredible.

Watching as she assembled another tower, he made a decision. As long as Ismena wanted him to stay, he would. Given half the chance, Nye would be glad to see the back of him, and his position as right-hand man to the leader of the London vampires was replaceable. He could already see Reed as a fine candidate, though he was still rather green.

Yes, it was a fine idea. As long as Ismena wanted him, he would do what he could to help the little witch. Her life would be an uphill battle all the way, and if he could alleviate some of the pressure on her, then he would.

Yes, he would stay.

Isobel stared at the scene unfolding before her and shook her head in surprise.

A thousand-year-old vampire was sitting on the floor piecing together building blocks with her two-week-old daughter, who was now a very well-developed two-year-old.

"Isobel," Nye said, appearing out of thin air behind her.

"Shh," she murmured, waving her hand at him. "Come look at this."

Nye leaned over her shoulder, and when he saw what was happening, a low growl sounded in his throat. He went to stride forward—probably to rip Tristan a new one for being alone in the same room as his daughter—but she pressed her palm against his chest.

"Don't," she whispered.

"Isobel. He disappeared for weeks and arrived just in time to witness the birth. Now he's in there alone with Ismena. Forgive me if I'm overprotective."

"She's perceptive, Nye. She knows his heart and wouldn't be in there if she sensed danger in him."

"How do you know? We don't even know what she's capable of. We don't even know..." he trailed off, not wanting to voice their greatest fear.

"You can't deny the things she's been doing," she argued. "I trust her, and now I trust him. Tristan is one of us and always has been. He's been questioning his place here ever since he was compelled. Right now, seeing Ismena playing with him without a care? He's got a place, and it's right here with us."

"I never liked his smugness," Nye said sullenly.

She elbowed him in the stomach. "He's not smug."

"He's a know-it-all."

Isobel sighed, knowing she would never win this argument with Nye. The spy had always had a rivalry with the knight, or at least, that's what she understood from the bits and pieces he'd told her in the last few months.

"She's going to grow up within the year," she said, voicing her thoughts. "She'll have the weight of the supernatural world on her shoulders whether she wants it or not. She's going to need all of us, Nye. She might have infinite power and knowledge, but somehow, I don't think it lends itself very well to social skills. Magic, yes. Making friends?" She shook her head, worrying about her little girl's future.

"Dad, Dad, Dad!" Ismena cried when she saw them standing in the doorway.

Tristan glanced up at them, his smile beginning to fade, and Isobel nodded, letting him know she was completely fine with their current arrangement.

Nye sighed and strode into the room. "What do we have here?" he declared, surveying her creation.

"Block!" she cried and then pointed to Tristan. "Tritan!" She tugged on Nye's trouser leg until he was forced to sit beside her.

Isobel smiled, a laugh escaping her lips as she watched the two big, bad vampires playing with the little redheaded witch.

Yeah, she was pretty sure they'd be okay.

For now.

Chapter 17

Gabby sat by the fireplace in the study, flipping through one of the grimoires from the bookshelf behind her.

The weeks were starting to fly by, and Ismena was still growing faster than she'd anticipated. Her search for answers had been fruitless, her list of questions growing with each passing day. There was no record of a child like this ever being born before. It was literally unheard of.

Alex heaved a sigh of frustration as he flipped through another tome that belonged to Regulus's collection of grimoires. She didn't know why he was helping since he couldn't read witch speak, but he was just as devoted to his niece as they all were.

Nye sat behind the desk, tending to his empire in brooding silence, completing the picture of awkwardness they currently sat in.

"Ismena's downstairs with Tristan," Isobel said, entering the room. "They'll be occupied for hours."

"Entrapment," Alex said with an amused smile. "Tristan is her new favourite toy. She forces him to go everywhere with her."

"At least he's being tortured," Nye quipped, earning himself a slap on the arm from Isobel. "What? Have you seen him with that little pink plastic pony? I've got photos."

She perched on the edge of the desk and smiled. "Oh, I know you do, but I've got videos."

"You do?" the spy asked, sitting up straight. Holding out his hand he gestured for her to give him the phone. "I want to see."

Gabby laughed and shook her head. It was a good feeling seeing her friends so lighthearted after everything that had happened in the last few months. Kidnappings, wraiths, rituals, being hunted by werewolves, reanimated corpses attacking the house, her poor wilted garden, arguing with the ancestor spirits...the list went on. The biggest surprise of all had been the arrival of little Ismena, who wasn't quite so little anymore.

A month had passed since the birth, and the newborn had unfurled and sprouted into a four-year-old girl. She was the image of her father with her mother's colouring, and it was becoming clearer every day. Ismena was going to be a beauty with the weight of the entire world on her shoulders.

She'd spent as much time as she was able to with the little witch, testing her abilities and teaching her spells and tricks. She could read the spells in Gabby's grimoire but didn't need them at all. She could grow a simple flower in her palm without much thought at all. She could float in the air for a few seconds when she jumped. Objects had a habit of hovering around the room, and her spoon bent when she had a tantrum at the dinner table. Not to mention the fact she seemed to understand the depths of everyone's emotions. Tristan had told her Ismena had calmed his inner torment with a simple touch when she was only two weeks old.

"Everything she does is instinctive," Gabby said, voicing her thoughts. "She doesn't need a spell to follow, and she doesn't need herbs or elixirs. She just does things. I've never seen anything like it."

"So none of that salt and pepper shit you put everywhere?" Nye asked with a smirk. "I'm forever finding it all over my paperwork."

"You have paperwork?" Isobel asked with a frown.

"I'm trying to imagine what she'll be like when she's all grown up and what she'll do, but I can't picture it," Alex mused.

"Give it another seventeen weeks," Nye said, flipping a gold letter opener over and over in his hand. "Then she'll be twenty-one. Just thank your lucky stars we don't have to suffer through a decade of teenageitis."

"Growing up is meant to be the fun part," Isobel grumbled. "The milestones..."

"I don't know what it's like now, but growing up was harsh and pitiful when I was a boy," the spy said. "If you grew up at all."

"You can hardly compare the Middle Ages to now," Gabby said, rolling her eyes. "So not the same thing."

"Yeah, there's a thing called healthcare," Alex said. "People live longer, and they grow taller."

"Watch yourself," Nye spat. "You may be a founder, Alex, but it doesn't give you permission to call me short."

"The way you're acting, maybe you should be the one downstairs playing with pink plastic ponies with Ismena," Isobel said. "Tristan would actually offer some useful advice instead of picking fights."

"There is no advice," Nye said, flipping the letter opener again. "There is only one day at a time."

"He's right, I'm afraid," Gabby said, closing the grimoire and placing it on the little table beside her.

"See?" the spy quipped, winking at Isobel.

"You're lucky you're handsome," she retorted.

"Otherwise?"

Isobel tried to hide her smile. "Otherwise, I'd get Gabby to bar you from coming inside the house."

"Everyone has referred to her as the Immortal Witch," Gabby said, attempting to get the conversation back on track. "Ismena, the original one, said it herself.

She'll grow up to a certain point, and there, she'll remain."

"If her destiny is to resurrect the Unhallowed, then what happens after that?" Alex asked, scratching his head. "What happens to someone after they fulfil the purpose of their existence?"

That was a deep question Gabby didn't know the answer to, but she suspected Ismena's destiny was twofold depending on which path she chose. It always came back to the light or the dark, no matter which way she shaped their predicament in her mind.

The others had thrown around wild suggestions that the little witch would cease to be once she'd expelled her power and that Eleanor planned to siphon her like a battery or even use her as a sacrifice. All of them were their greatest fears, but all were the most extreme. Gabby didn't want to believe any of them were even a possibility.

If she could find a way to get the power herself, she could spare Ismena from becoming involved at all and do the job herself. Then Ismena's destiny would change entirely, and there would be yet another path for her to follow.

"They just go on, I suppose," she replied. "I doubt people drop dead the moment they realise their life's work is complete."

"Besides, Ismena's destiny isn't to resurrect that cow Eleanor and her bitchy coven. Not anymore," Isobel said with a pout. "Her destiny is a much happier one. I won't have it any other way."

Nye's cell phone began to ring, and he pulled it out of his pocket, glancing at the screen. Answering the call with a brisk, "What," he exited the room.

"So all we can do is watch and wait?" Alex asked. "There's nothing we can do?"

Gabby shook her head. There wasn't.

"The best thing we can possibly do is everything we've already been doing. Care for her, teach her, love her."

"And wait for Eleanor to rear her ugly head." Alex glanced at Gabby, an unasked question lingering in his eyes.

Gabby turned away, her mind turning to the task ahead. How they were going to defeat the Unhallowed without using Ismena's power was beyond her, but there was no other option. She had to find a way. She had to.

Leaving the study, Gabby found Nye out in the hall, pacing back and forth, talking furiously on his phone.

When he saw the witch, he cut the call and shoved his phone back into his pocket.

"Don't stop on my account," she said, raising an eyebrow. "I've got bigger fish to fry than whatever infighting between vampire gangs you're attempting to squash."

"For once, there's none of that," Nye said. "Shock horror."

"That would have to be a first."

"After Ismena was born, I sent the Six out to track the wraith," he said, glancing over his shoulder toward the stairs. The faint sounds of Ismena's happy chattering floated up from the living room, a constant reminder of what was at stake.

"Have they found anything?" Gabby asked.

"Nothing," he replied, gritting his teeth. "It's like she disappeared into thin air."

"I'm not surprised. She's biding her time. Waiting for the right moment."

"Which is?"

She shrugged. "I'm winging this just as much as you are."

"All I can see on our horizon is a huge pile of wraith shit," Nye said, glaring at her. "I won't let her take Ismena, but I'm not sure I'll have a choice. Tell me you've got an idea, Gabby. Doesn't matter how farfetched it is, I'll do whatever it takes."

Nye was ready to sacrifice himself for his daughter? The shocks just kept coming these days.

"I'd like to say I've got something, but I haven't," she said.

"What about your ghost buddies?" he asked. "They were awfully cheery when they gave Mena that diamond necklace. It saved her once, so maybe it can save her again.”

Gabby shook her head. “No, it doesn’t work like that. It’s not a weapon. It’s merely for her protection. It saved her once, but I’m not sure it will again now that Eleanor has seen it. Right now, we need something to end the threat altogether.”

“Gabby, I hate to put all of this on you, but I don’t know what else to do.”

She laughed, attempting to alleviate some of the stress that was weighing them all down. “Nye Saer, admitting he’s indebted to a witch? It must be a miracle.”

“No playing around,” he hissed. “This has to end. That little girl has enough to deal with without a psycho out to get her. If there’s a way to send that bitch to hell without getting Mena involved, then we’ve got to do it. That kid doesn’t deserve to be used.”

Gabby bowed her head, grateful Nye was on the same page.

“I have an idea,” she said. “But I have to meditate on it.”

“Let me know if you need anything,” the spy said, grasping her shoulder. It was as close as he’d come to hugging her, so she took the gesture as a welcome one even though he was glaring at her quite threateningly.

Without another word, she moved around him and ventured downstairs, stepping out into the garden.

It still pained her to see the grounds looking like a

desolate wasteland, but when she passed the patch of earth she'd been using to teach Ismena how to grow flowers, she smiled. The little plot was filled with daisies, their yellow centres a welcome burst of colour among the darkness.

Standing before Regulus's olive tree, she stared up at the branches covered in green leaves and olives that were ripe for the picking. When she grew it the night they buried the Roman, she'd ensured it would stand tall and bear fruit for eons, a symbol of the strength the founding vampire had carried with him through the ages. Now the tree bore the symbol of his legacy.

A soft tugging drew Gabby's attention downward, and she frowned when she found Ismena beside her. She hadn't even heard the little witch approach, thinking she was still playing with Tristan in the house.

Ismena stared up at Gabby, her hazel eyes sparkling. Glancing at the olive tree, she scrunched up her nose and sniffed. Then she grasped Gabby's hand.

"Love," she said, pointing to the tree.

Then as suddenly as she'd appeared, the little witch ran off across the yard, skipping into the house like nothing had happened.

"She's a curious little thing."

Gabby jumped, clutching her heart at the sound of Reed's voice. "What's with all the sneaking around this place?"

"No sneaking," the vampire said, standing beside

her. "I saw you out here and wanted to check if you needed anything today."

"Aren't you meant to be out searching for Eleanor with the Six?"

"Yes," he nodded, suddenly looking a lot like Tristan. "I'm on my way inside to give Nye my report."

"Which is?"

"The same as yesterday," he replied with a frown. "I wish I had better news."

"Don't we all," she declared with a sigh.

Reed shifted closer. "Are you well?"

"As I can be." Was she well? What kind of question was that? Of course, she wasn't, but there was no medicine she could take for what ailed her. "And you?"

He smiled and shook his head. She knew he hadn't confessed his parentage to Tristan—his long-lost father—since the night they fought side by side to fend off Eleanor. They'd all been on edge, but time was running out. Dumb luck would only get them so far, and she knew they couldn't rely on it, not anymore. They needed a foolproof plan, or they were all going to die, and Ismena would be used to resurrect an evil coven of wraiths. They were the last line of defence.

"You need to speak to him, Reed," she said. "Eleanor is coming back for Ismena, and we might not be as lucky as last time. If you're going to say something, I would do it now."

"Perhaps," he said, a note of sadness in his voice.

She stared at him for a long moment, watching his

changing expression, then said, "You had better deliver the bad news to Nye. Tristan is in the living room watching Ismena. Perhaps you can speak to him, at least, even if you don't confide your secret."

The vampire nodded once. "And you? Do you require assistance?"

"No, I'm fine." She gestured to the tree, which would act as her doorway to the other side in lieu of a living garden around her. "I need to do this part alone."

Reed smiled and left, disappearing into the house to face Nye's displeasure. She hoped he would talk to his father and tell him the truth. God knew Tristan needed something to live for.

Reed stood in the foyer of the Hampstead mansion, smarting from bearing the brunt of Nye Saer's displeasure.

A vampire being able to hunt a wraith was just as absurd as a baby who grew a year in a week. One of those things had happened, so there must be a miracle waiting when it came to the other. Anything was better than returning tomorrow with the same news he'd been delivering for the past month.

Hesitating at the entrance to the living room, he saw Tristan clearing up the mess of toys the child witch had left in her wake. It was such a strange sight to see a thousand-year-old vampire, his father, tidy up the mess of a four-year-old girl.

"Where is the little one?" he asked, drawing the knight's attention. "Gabby said you were watching her."

"Gone for lunch with Isobel," Tristan replied, placing the last of the building blocks back into their bright yellow container.

As he watched the knight, Reed wondered if he'd done the same for his sister Annabelle when she was that small. Perhaps he hadn't since his mother had told him he'd been away with the Knights Templar a great deal. His fortune and station in the order had kept them from begging on the street, so they'd borne the absence, but for Reed... Well, he wouldn't know since Tristan had supposedly died in a faraway land and had never known he had a son at all.

Taking the small leather-bound copy of the Bible from his pocket, Reed turned it over in his hand, ashamed he'd stolen it from Tristan's room the night he and Gabby discovered the knight had left. He'd just wanted something that had been his father's, but now he saw it had been the wrong thing to do. Desperation had guided his hand.

"Is that..." Tristan rose to his feet, having seen the book.

Now was as good a time as any, he supposed. What would be the worst thing that happened? Tristan refusing to believe him, forcing him to go back on the road alone. He was tired of wondering if there was anything else out there for him other than being alone.

"You can't tell me you don't see her in me," he said, handing Tristan the Bible.

Tristan stared at him, his brow furrowed.

"Juliette," he said.

The knight's brow furrowed, his eyes carrying a warning.

"Reed isn't my real name," he said, going for it. "It was just an identity I took after I turned."

"What is your name?" the knight asked carefully, his voice full of trepidation.

"Aedan," he muttered, casting his gaze away. "Aedan na Tri Tor."

"Explain yourself," Tristan hissed. "What kind of trick are you playin' at?"

"I am long past the time for tricks," he spat. "I've searched for you for nearly eight hundred years. I thought you long gone, but here you are. You are my father, and I am the son you never knew you had, put in my mother's belly before you marched to your death. Had you come home..." he trailed off, his jaw tensing.

"I didn't come home," the knight declared. "I couldn't."

"I understand," Reed began. "I thought you'd died, just like everyone else. It wasn't until later I found out the truth."

"My son," the knight began, shaking his head in disbelief. "I had a son."

"*Have*," Reed said firmly, beginning to regret he'd said anything at all.

They stared at one another in silence, and he didn't dare move in case Tristan changed his mind and decided he didn't want to believe.

"How did it happen?" he finally asked. "How did you turn?"

"I was twenty-seven," Reed began. "I was a soldier just like you'd been. I never became a knight, not by a long shot, but I guess you can understand why that was."

Tristan nodded.

Reed grimaced. "Declared the hero of Constantinople and branded traitor all on the same day. It had a lasting legacy."

"If you'd seen the disgusting' things they were doin' to the civilians of that city and others just like it... Rapin' and pillagin' in the name of God. I could not stand for it a moment longer. I was the one who got inside and opened the gate to let the army in. I stood up to them and was sent to my death in the sewers underneath the city. If you're truly a son of mine, you would have done the same thing."

"We were sent to Normandy to squash a rebellion against the Crown. The French were in support of the usurpers..."

"You died in battle?"

"For years I'd dealt with the torment of being a traitor's son even though I never knew you. It wasn't the enemy who slew me but men who were supposed to be brothers in arms. During the battle against the rebels, they set upon me. An easy way to deliver death without blame coming back on them." Reed shrugged. "I don't know how vampire blood came to be in my system and no one else's, but I was alone."

"Vampires were known to lurk around battlefields," Tristan said gently. "Perhaps you were fed upon, healed, and then compelled to forget."

"Perhaps. I woke hours later in a field of corpses with a ravenous hunger."

"Then what happened?"

"I dragged myself back to camp. It was night, the darkness absolute. The men who slew me were horrified to see me standing there. I remembered their swords as they gutted me. I remembered their callous laughter. I remembered it all. I killed them where they stood with my bare hands. I ripped into their throats with my teeth...and so it was done." He waited for Tristan to say something, but he remained silent, likely testing him to see if his story rang true within his own conscious. "A long time passed, I toiled and struggled with what I'd become, and then I heard about you. I searched ever since, but it wasn't until..."

"Until?"

"I came to London and heard you were working with Regulus."

Tristan stared at him, unblinking. *Goddammit, say something!*

"So you see, you do have something to live for."

Tristan stared at him, his expression clear, and Reed began to fidget, not knowing what his father thought of him. Finding out he had a son after a thousand years of wandering, thinking he was alone in the world? He supposed it was a great deal to take in.

"After Eleanor compelled me, it changed somethin' inside me," the knight began. "I've struggled with my path in this world from the day I was born. As a human, and then as a vampire. I began this life killin' and slaughterin' innocents, and I've worked to atone for it ever since. I will be for the rest of my days. I've never belonged anywhere, not really."

"Not even with Mother and Annabelle?"

Tristan smiled, his eyes misting. "It's been a long time since I heard her name. Annabelle. Juliette." Then he shook his head, thinking about Reed's question. "I regret that I never had much time with them. It was the way of things back then, as you know. Long years away on campaigns saw me apart from them more than I would have liked, but I had to provide a wage. Otherwise, they would have been forced out of our home."

"And Grandfather had cast us off long before I was born," Reed added.

"Aye, that he did. Do you know what became of them?"

Reed nodded. "They believed me dead, and I allowed them to mourn me, knowing they'd never accept what I'd become of their own free will. I checked in on them over the years. Mother lived a long life, and Annabelle married a merchant from the midlands. They moved away from the city and went on as well as they could."

"Juliette..."

"Never remarried."

Tristan sighed, his thoughts still remaining his own.

"And now?" Reed asked. "Do we continue as we were, or..."

He'd finally found the courage to reveal his identity to his father, but after all this time, did he actually want him? He'd been forced to become the very thing Tristan hated about himself—a bloodthirsty vampire —so would he want a relationship with him, knowing he would be looking in the mirror and seeing everything he abhorred every single day?

"Yes," the knight said after a moment. "We continue. If I have learned anythin' in this life, it is that the future remains ours. We can only come to terms with what we have done and do our best to right them. You are a part of this now Reed, how could I not want to know my own blood?" Picking up Ismena's pink pony, he smiled. "What a strange family we have become."

Reed stared at the plastic toy and shook his head in

bewilderment. He'd wanted to find his father since the day he learned he was still alive, but never in his wildest dreams did he imagine he would be inheriting not only Tristan but the group of mismatched supernaturals who lived in the manor, too.

What a family, indeed.

Chapter 18

Gabby opened her eyes, her body stiff from the hours she'd been sitting on the hard earth, meditating.

The sun had already begun setting, twilight well and truly blanketing the city. Her joints were stiff, but her mind was clear.

Staring up at the olive tree, she knew exactly what she was meant to do. Sifting through the dreams and memories of a thousand witches and creatures who had departed to the other side had taken its toll, but an answer had presented itself. An answer she'd known all along but hadn't wanted to acknowledge.

All this time, she was avoiding the truth because she wanted to save something of herself, her dreams of a future too alluring for her to even consider another option. The ultimate sacrifice.

She'd have to turn to darkness herself to defeat the

Unhallowed. Give up her goodness to the coil of poison in her soul, siphon the ley lines and use the strength of the earth to shatter the wraiths on both sides of the veil once and for all. It was a betrayal of her own kind, and the ancestor spirits would likely shun her for all eternity, but she would do it regardless.

Would she survive the ordeal? Was there a way back from so much pain and suffering? She'd almost been overwhelmed by it once, all that time ago when the Roman founder Arturius had taken her and attempted to turn her into his evil puppet. Aya had been able to bring her back from the brink, but this time...she'd have to dive right off the edge.

Gabby knew there wasn't a way back from the abyss even as her mind mulled over a way around it. It was a suicide mission, plain and simple. The others couldn't know her plan, or they would try to stop her. This was the only way.

Thinking of Ismena, she knew she would do it to spare the little girl the suffering. She was an innocent and didn't deserve the fate brought upon her by Eleanor's meddling with nature.

Standing, she cast one more look at the olive tree before walking away. Would she see Regulus on the other side? Perhaps she might. It was a comforting thought, knowing her final hours were upon her.

She stepped into the kitchen, and Alex raised his head from the newspaper he was reading at the island.

"Gabby?" he asked, catching her arm. "Are you okay? You were out there for ages."

"I have a plan," she said, waving him off. "Get Nye and Tristan, and meet me in the study."

His eyebrows rose. "A plan to kill Eleanor?"

"Bring the others," she said firmly, making a beeline for the study.

Clattering up the stairs, she shoved into the study and went straight to the bookshelves, ignoring Nye who was sitting behind the desk, his cell phone to his ear. At her abrupt entrance, he ended the call and watched her closely.

He raised his eyebrows as she rummaged through the shelves, looking for that grimoire she'd found with the dark spells inside. From the condition it was in, Regulus must have taken it from a dark witch sometime during the Middle Ages. All torn and stained with ancient blood, the pages thick and made from pulped reeds. It emanated a particular stench, but there were many similar artefacts in here that shared the same aura.

"What's up your ass?" the spy asked.

"I've got a plan," she muttered, finally locating the grimoire and flipping through the pages.

"You're shitting me," he exclaimed, rising to his feet. "All that sitting around in the garden finally paid off?"

"Meditation," she snapped, finding the page she was looking for—the process she hoped to follow to allow her to siphon the ley lines. "I was sifting through memories of the spirits."

"Sounds like a trip."

"Don't be a smartass," Alex said, stepping into the study, followed closely by Tristan.

"Forgive me if I'm skeptical," the spy drawled. "After months of 'stuffed if I know' reports from all you sods, I'm not about to get my hopes up only to have to rip apart someone's coronary artery to vocalise my displeasure."

"Way harsh," the founder spat.

"What's going on?" Isobel asked, barging in after the vampires. "Alex said you have a plan?"

Gabby nodded, thankful for the interruption. Bickering vampires wasn't going to help with this. "I do, but no one is going to like it."

"Spill already," Nye said, rolling his eyes. "I'm about done with all the uncertainty and waiting. I need to do something."

"We need to take the fight to Eleanor," she said.

"Where?" Alex asked.

She raised an eyebrow. "Where else?"

"The standing stones?" Nye asked. "But that's where she's most powerful."

She nodded. "But it will be where I'm most powerful, too."

"What do you mean? Last time, you didn't have enough power..."

"I almost did," she countered. "I managed to

overwhelm four out of the five. Whatever essence they had left, they gave to Eleanor, making her stronger and more powerful than she was the first time around. I felt it the night Ismena was born. I faltered then, as well. I have a way to stand strong and get the power I need to withstand Eleanor's assault."

Isobel faltered, her gaze flickering to Nye. "She means to siphon the ley lines. That's what you mean, right?"

"But that's dark magic," the spy exclaimed. "Everything you stand against. Using dark magic is what created the Unhallowed in the first place. You can't be serious."

Gabby remained steadfast in her plan. "Sometimes, we have to do bad things in order to save what's good in the world."

"What do you need?" Nye asked, causing Isobel to balk.

"You're just going to let her turn to dark magic?"

"There's no other way. If there was, we'd have found it a long time ago," he replied.

"He's right," Gabby said gravely. "Not even the ancestor spirits knew. Ismena—the founding witch—didn't know, either."

Isobel shook her head in disbelief. "No!"

"What do you need?" Nye asked, ignoring Isobel. "Whatever it is, consider it done."

"Time," Gabby replied. "We'll need to go to the standing stones where Eleanor performed the ritual on you. The ley lines will be open to me there, making it easier to siphon. Considering I haven't done this before, I'll need some help. Someone to watch over me."

"There are three vampires here who are strong enough to face a wraith," Tristan said, breaking his silence.

"You would face Eleanor?" she asked. "After what she did to you?"

"She has no power over me," he replied, inclining his head. "Only my own mind keeps me from fighting."

"He's a regular Obi-Wan fucking Kenobi," Nye said with a roll of his eyes.

"Once I tap into the ley lines, Eleanor will be alerted to our presence," Gabby continued, ignoring the spy. "That's where the time comes in."

"Then we'll buy it for you," Alex said. "Fend her off until you're ready."

"What about Ismena?" Isobel asked.

Nye raised his eyebrows. "What about her? This is a magical fight, Isobel. You'll stay here with her."

"Oh, is that right?"

"He's right, Izzy," Alex said. "She needs her parents, or at worst, one of them."

Gesturing to Tristan, Nye said, "We need a fourth."

"Reed," he said. "I trust no other."

Gabby peered at the knight and cocked her head to the side, an unanswered question passing between them. He nodded once, and that was all she needed to know. Reed had told him the truth, and it had been a good outcome.

"Then get him here immediately," the spy commanded. "We leave as soon as Gabby has made her preparations."

"But..." Isobel began but was cut off when Nye pulled her into his arms and placed a kiss on her lips.

"We're doing this for Ismena," he said. "She's the most important of all. If this goes bad, then she'll need her mother by her side. We can't leave her alone in this world."

"You think this is going to—"

"Shh," he crooned.

"There's always a risk," Gabby said kindly. "We have to be prepared."

"What if the dark magic corrupts you like it did to the Unhallowed?" Izzy asked, looking panicked. "How can we get you back?"

"It won't," she replied, knowing full well it already lived inside her. Maybe this was what it was for all this time. Perhaps this was her destiny after all.

"But—"

"She'll be okay, Iz," Alex said as Nye embraced her. "She knows what she's doing.

Glancing at Isobel with a heavy heart, Gabby said, "We had better begin."

Isobel watched on as the vampires began amassing in the living room.

She stood in the foyer beside the ten million pounds worth of Michelangelo painting hanging on the wall while Alex, Tristan, Reed, Nye, and the witch Gabby all prepared for battle with Eleanor. She wanted to go and fight, to protect her daughter and the world from the Unhallowed, but what power did she have? None at all.

Nye was right. She was useless. He didn't exactly say it, but she knew he'd thought it.

"What are they doing?"

She glanced down at Ismena, startled by the change in her voice. It only felt like that morning that she was still speaking her words with dropped letters, her tongue still having trouble with the letter *s*. Now she seemed to have a complete grasp of the English language...and looked exactly like an eight-year-old girl.

"They're going to run an errand," she replied.

"Are you angry?"

Isobel's exterior melted, and she knelt before Ismena, smoothing her fingers through her daughter's hair.

"Not at all," she said. "I wanted to go too, but...I can't."

The little witch studied her with her strange honey coloured eyes. "Why not?"

"Because I'm here with you."

Ismena watched the group in the living room for a moment, then narrowed her eyes. Leaning close, she whispered in Isobel's ear, "Aunt Gabby is going to do a bad thing."

Isobel drew back, startled. "What do you mean?"

"She has a bad shadow inside her, and she wants to use it against the lady."

"Mena," Isobel said, beginning to worry she'd overheard something they'd been trying to save her from. "Gabby doesn't have a bad shadow inside her."

"Yes, she does. I can see it."

Isobel glanced into the living room at Gabby, wondering what Ismena meant. She knew Gabby intended to use dark spells to siphon the ley lines to use against Eleanor, but what was the dark shadow inside her? Did she already have dark power at her disposal?

"Can you see it now?" she asked her daughter. "The shadow?"

She looked at Gabby and nodded.

"You're worried about Aunt Gabby, aren't you?"

Ismena nodded again, this time more furiously. "It will eat her up."

Isobel's smile faded, and an alarming sense of foreboding overcame her senses. Gabby had said it herself. The spirits had told her Ismena would have infinite knowledge. Had she been able to tap into that part of herself yet? She didn't know, but she knew if she didn't listen to her daughter now, she'd be making a huge mistake.

"Do you want to go?" Ismena whispered. "I can hide us."

"*Mena*," she scolded.

"Aunt Gabby can't use the shadow," she declared. "The shadow will eat her all up."

Isobel's heart began to pound as she realised the gravity of Gabby's plan. Did her friend know what would happen to her if she managed to defeat Eleanor? The toll would be too great...

Gabby was sacrificing herself to spare Ismena from using her power. Isobel wanted the same thing, to spare her daughter from becoming a tool, but not at the cost of her friend's life. Was this truly the only way?

"I can do it, Mommy," she said. "I followed the light."

"The light?" Isobel asked, attempting to see what exactly Ismena understood about her destiny.

"I was made from magic. Aunt Gabby says I have lots of it. I know she gets tired when she uses hers, but I never do. She said I should follow the light and protect all the good things that live on the planet like you and Daddy. Daddy is a vampire, and vampires are supposed to be bad, but he's a good vampire. Just like Uncle Tristan." She puffed out her chest. "I can protect Aunt Gabby from the lady, and then the shadow won't eat her up."

"You can?" Isobel asked. "Are you sure, sweetie?"

She nodded furiously. "Daddy won't let us go, but we can hide. Do you know Harry Potter? He has an invisibility cloak!"

Well, there was one normal thing about her daughter. She was obsessed with Harry Potter just like every kid her age.

"You can hide us like that?" she asked. "Daddy has super hearing, you know."

Ismena nodded. "He won't hear."

Isobel thought over it a moment, knowing she had to make a decision right now, or they would miss their chance to hitch a ride to the standing stones. Ismena was so certain she could protect them from Eleanor, who she called 'the lady.' If Gabby truly intended to sacrifice her life in order to save them all, including sparing Ismena from using her power, then the cost was too great. Mena was still a child, but she understood, and she could help. She was offering. Surely that was different than forcing her to face the Unhallowed?

"Daddy's going to be really angry," she said with a frown.

"He'll be okay," Mena said, not at all worried about getting into trouble.

Isobel smiled and kissed her on her forehead. "Then hide us."

She grasped her daughter's hand and led her through the kitchen and into the garage where the car was waiting. Hoping she was making the right decision, she opened the trunk and lifted her daughter inside.

"Remember, invisibility cloaks on, and no sound, okay?"

Ismena nodded, looking pleased as punch as Isobel squeezed into the trunk beside her and closed them inside.

Chapter 19

Nye watched on as Gabby stood over the Blood Stone, the same stone he'd lain on during Eleanor's ritual.

The power that had ripped through his body and poured directly into the wraiths had been overwhelming, the voices tearing at his mind only adding to his agony. To think he'd been privy to the murmurings of the earth. Was that what it felt like to be a witch like Gabby? Maybe, but perhaps not quite as painful.

The ritual had been twofold, acting as a way to mask the spell that had made him fertile and to tether him to the ley lines so the Unhallowed could siphon more power than they'd ever had before.

Standing in the place that had caused him so much agony was difficult, but if everything went according to plan, then by sunrise, Eleanor and her psycho pack of wraiths would be no more.

As soon as they'd arrived at the standing stones, they'd illuminated a new set of torches, sticking the long poles into the shredded earth—the calling card Gabby had left behind on her last visit—and creating a perimeter around the witch as she lined herself to the ley lines running beneath them.

Gabby's plan was simple. Stand vigil as she siphoned as she would be vulnerable until she was at maximum energy, then back her up when Eleanor finally appeared. She would do most of the work...and yet again, all their problems could only be solved by a witch. The thought annoyed Nye more than he'd even admit aloud, but his hands were tied. He'd struggled with the notion of becoming a father, but Ismena had become more to him that he ever thought possible. He'd lick Gabby's boots if he had to, and if this would save his little witch, then he'd lick until they shone.

Nye let his mind wander as his hearing stretched out over the field and to the motorway beyond. Nothing moved over the landscape, but the harder he listened, the more he was able to pick out the faint thrumming of what sounded like a twin heartbeat. *Thump thump, thump thump.*

Glancing at the others, they didn't seem to hear it, so he gestured to Tristan that he was going to check the perimeter. If it was Eleanor coming out to play, then Gabby would have sensed her and alerted them. It must be a stray animal, and if it was human, he'd compel them to give this place a wide berth. They didn't need any added complications tonight.

Stepping out of the ring of firelight, he followed the sound across the field, his footsteps following the path they'd created during their approach to the stone circle. When the car came into view, his irritation rose as he realised the sound was coming from inside. Probably some punk kid attempting to hot-wire the sedan. Seriously? Car thieves out in the middle of nowhere? This had to be some kind of sick joke.

Shoving his hand into his pocket, he pressed the unlock button on the keys, and the indicators flashed. Flinging open the boot, Nye growled in anger as Ismena sat up, her fiery red hair a complete mess. Isobel followed suit, looking sheepish.

"Seriously?" he exclaimed.

"Hi, Daddy!" Ismena chortled.

"What do you think you're doing?" he growled.

"Aunt Gabby wants to use the bad thing inside her," Ismena said, not at all perturbed by her father's displeasure.

He narrowed his eyes and glanced at Isobel, looking for answers.

"She's very convincing," she declared as their daughter scrambled out of the boot and landed lithely on the ground.

"Daddy," Ismena said, tugging on his hand. "She can't stop the bad lady."

Nye glanced at Isobel with a frown, then knelt before his daughter. "What do you mean, Mena?" he asked. "What bad lady?"

"The wraith lady," she replied.

Nye turned his attention back to Isobel, who was ungracefully climbing out of the boot. "What did you say to her?"

"Nothing," she retorted, dusting herself off.

"Mommy didn't say anything," Ismena declared. "I heard lots of times." She picked up the diamond pendant from around her neck. "I saw her, too. I heard lots of voices in the dark, and then I saw you, Daddy. Then Mommy. You were scared of the lady, but you don't have to be."

"Do I want to ask any more questions?" Nye asked Isobel.

She shook her head. "I don't think there's a way around this, Nye. Gabby is going on a suicide mission." She glanced at Ismena, who was clutching his knees. "She understands more than we ever realised. She's only a child, but I trust her. She can help."

"She doesn't understand," he said firmly.

"Yes, she does. She knows what's happening. She might not be able to articulate it, but I can see it."

Nye wasn't convinced. "You can see it?"

"I can't explain it, but she knows and wants to help."

The spy narrowed his eyes and glanced at Ismena,

studying her features. "And what do you have to say for yourself, young lady?"

"I can help Aunt Gabby," she said defiantly. "I'm a special witch. A good witch. I don't want her to use the shadow."

"The shadow? Well, it's too late," he said, glancing at the standing stones. "She's already siphoning."

Ismena let out a startled gasp and took off across the field, running through the grass that came up to her chest. With a roll of his eyes, Nye ran forward, catching the little girl with ease. He lifted her into his arms and carried her the rest of the way with Isobel bringing up the rear.

The moment they stepped into the firelight, all eyes were on them. Gabby's attention was brought back to the present, her mouth falling open.

"Ismena?" she asked. "What..."

"Don't, Aunt Gabby," Ismena said, squirming in Nye's arms.

"They stowed away in the boot," Nye explained, setting her down. "Cunning little thing must've used a cloaking spell."

"Oh, Mena," Gabby said with a sigh.

"Change of plans," Nye said to the assembled vampires. "Protect Ismena at all costs. There's no stopping this now. We have to see it through."

"But..." Ismena complained.

"Shh," Isobel said, smoothing her hand through the little witch's hair. "We'll just watch and wait, okay?"

"Well, well, well, isn't this just something." A malicious voice echoed through the darkness, breaking apart the group. "A perfect little family about to be torn apart. How *fake* it all is."

Eleanor stepped into the firelight, causing the three vampires to form a line before Nye, Isobel, and Ismena. Her hair was wild, her curls framing her pale face, her eyes crackling with a storm of siphoned earth energy.

"She's darling," the wraith cooed, her gaze falling on Ismena. "She looks just like her father and that hair... Positively vibrant."

"You'll stay the hell away from her," Alex snarled, baring his fangs. "She doesn't belong to you. She's not a tool for you to manipulate."

"This one is so...cute," the wraith declared, her lip curling. "Thinking because he's a founder, he has a chance. *How arrogant.*"

"Alex, watch out!" Isobel cried, but it was too late.

The wraith flicked her wrist, sending the founder flying. He collided with one of the standing stones on the outer circle, his neck snapping. The vampire's head lolled to the side, his body pinned at the pinnacle of the stone.

Tristan came at Eleanor from behind, and she turned, snarling at the knight, flinging him just as easily as she had Alex. His body slammed against another stone, his head twisting to the side. Their bodies didn't desiccate, which meant they were still alive. In Alex's case, there was no doubt he would survive, but Tristan was another story.

Nye scooped up Ismena in his arms and held her close, shielding her from the wraith.

"Thank you for delivering everyone in one nice little package, Gabrielle," Eleanor said with a triumphant smirk. "I was wondering how long it would take you to realise you had to sacrifice yourself in order to save them. Unfortunately, nothing you do will stop me. No matter how much power you siphon, the only thing you'll end up being is the thing you loathe the most." She smiled, spreading her arms wide. "*Me.*"

"I wouldn't count on it," Gabby hissed.

Reed stepped forward, but the witch held out her hand, stopping him from going any further.

"Don't," Nye hissed at him. "Or you'll end up like the others."

Eleanor laughed, the sound of her voice loud in the silence. "That's the most intelligent thing I've heard you say since I came back." Her attention turned to Ismena, and she smiled. "You and I shall be together soon, darling. It is destined."

"Stay away from her," Isobel snapped, shifting her body between the wraith and her daughter.

Eleanor snarled and raised her hand. Isobel was dragged across the clearing by an invisible force, and she fell to her knees before the wraith, gasping for breath.

"She'll be mine the moment your bond has been

broken," she snarled. "Mother and father shall be no more, then all that is left is darkness...and I shall begin with you. The feeble human who dared to defy their superior!"

She pulled a dagger from behind her back, raising it high into the air. Beginning to chant, Eleanor's form started to flicker, her wraith essence breaking through into the physical realm. She was turning—and from being subjected to Gabby's incessant mutterings the past few months—Nye knew she would be at her most powerful the moment she transformed into her pure wraith form.

"Isobel!" Nye cried, unable to help her while he held Ismena. "Move!"

"I... I... I can't," she stammered. "I'm stuck."

"Let her go, you bitch!" Gabby let out a roar and stepped forward, her hands raised as she began chanting an incantation of her own.

As her words gained momentum, Nye could feel the air pulse with power, and the earth began to shake under his feet. Clutching Ismena tightly, he held his ground, Reed beside him. The vampire looked as if he wanted to spring forth, but he stood firmly, knowing his orders were to protect Ismena before everything else.

Eleanor shrieked in pain, her fists pounding against her head as whatever spell Gabby was hurling at her threw her concentration off. It was enough to break Isobel free, and she rose to her feet, stumbling backward, then she turned and ran.

Gabby threw her right hand back toward them while her other remained on Eleanor, and a shimmering veil began to descend. *A shield.* Isobel ran faster toward Nye and Ismena, her eyes wide with fear. *She wasn't going to make it.*

"Isobel, run!" Nye cried, his arms full with his child.

The shield slammed down, completely separating them, and Isobel ran into it, her fists pounding against the shimmering web.

"Mommy!" Ismena cried.

Gabby turned, faltering when she realised what had happened. It was all the time Eleanor needed to break free of her grasp, and she dissolved into thin air. The air fogged around Isobel, and the wraith appeared, the dagger raised to strike.

"Aunt Gabby!" Ismena cried, struggling against Nye's grasp. "Aunt Gabby, no!" She lunged, desperately reaching her hands out toward the witch.

Gabby faltered, her knees buckling beneath her. The barrier flickered and failed, the shimmering shield glowing brightly before disintegrating into nothing. As Gabby crumpled to the ground, Reed rushed forward and caught her in his arms.

"Mena," Nye asked the little girl. "What did you do?"

"*No!*" the little witch cried, tears running down her

face. "She was going to use the shadow. She was going to lock me away!"

He glanced at Gabby, but she was knocked out cold, Reed's jostling doing nothing to wake her. Eleanor smiled in triumph and closed the gap between her and Isobel, the dagger glinting in her hand. *He had to do something.*

"*Daddy, let me go!*" Ismena shrieked, the ground beginning to shift underneath them.

Nye glanced between her and Isobel, completely torn. Reed cradled Gabby in his arms, desperately trying to rouse her, Alex and Tristan were immobilised against the standing stones, and he held his daughter in his arms. Nothing stood between Eleanor and the woman he loved. Even if Ismena weren't there, he wouldn't be able to face the wraith, not without getting his neck snapped.

He knew what Isobel would tell him to do if she were capable of voicing her wishes. *Save Ismena.*

He took a step backward, cradling his daughter in his arms, and the movement caused her wailing to increase.

"Daddy, no!"

"I need to get you away from here," he murmured, his gaze falling to Isobel.

"No, no, no, *no!*"

Ismena began to squirm in Nye's grasp, the earth beginning to shudder violently beneath his feet. A sharp breeze stirred his hair, gaining momentum until it buffeted his body. She thrashed against his hold and eventually broke free, the little girl too cunning even with his vampire strength in play.

"Mena, no!" he cried, but the little witch wasn't listening. He ran forward, moving as fast as his vampire strength enabled him, but he was brought up short, his face smacking into an invisible barrier. "*Mena!*"

She ignored him, her power forcing him back, and she ran straight for Isobel and Eleanor, completely unafraid.

"*Mena!*"

Eleanor loomed over Isobel, a look of pure malice on her face, and raised her hand to strike…

This is it, Isobel thought. *This is how it all ends. Stabbed to death by a psycho wraith. Who saw that coming?*

Instinctively, she held up her arms to shield herself, but at the last second, Ismena appeared before her. Flinging her little body between the women, she stood defiantly in the face of the wraith, not even breaking stride.

"Go away!" she screamed, her tiny voice shrill in the storm of her own creation. "*Leave my mommy alone!*"

Eleanor's eyes widened, and she recoiled as if she'd

been slapped with an invisible power. "Darling," she cooed, dropping the dagger to her side. "I'm your true mother. You're destined to save a great number of people from a dark place. Did you know?"

Ismena turned, her gaze fixing on Isobel, who was dumbstruck by the turn of events. She raised her hand for her daughter. Whatever the little girl thought, she didn't know, but she ignored her mother's beckoning and turned back to Eleanor.

Her heart began to break. *No!*

"That's it, darling," the wraith murmured, gesturing for the little witch to follow.

Everyone froze, not knowing what to do. One misstep and Ismena could be torn from them forever, but if they did nothing... Tears began to stream from Isobel's eyes, her sobs bursting forth unchecked.

"Mena," she cried desperately. "Mommy loves you, you hear? Whatever you choose, Mommy loves you no matter what."

Suddenly, at the sound of her mother's voice, the little girl sprung to life.

"Go. *Away!*" Ismena threw her arms wide and screamed at Eleanor, her little body exploding with a light so bright, Isobel was forced to shield her eyes.

"No!" Eleanor cried. "You wouldn't dare!"

"Mena," Isobel sobbed. "Mena..."

The light intensified, and a silent burst of energy forced Isobel to fall flat to the ground. It was if a bomb had exploded above the stone circle. A bomb that was completely silent. Then just as suddenly as it began, it seemed to be over. The light began to fade and the night sky came back into view, the stars shining just as they always did.

Isobel blinked, her vision full of spots, and she pushed herself up off the ground, dazed and confused.

"Mena," she said through a moan. "Mena, where are you?"

"Mommy!" Little arms circled her neck, and a matching body flung itself into her lap.

"Oh, God, Mena!" she exclaimed, hugging her daughter. "Are you okay? Did she hurt you?"

Ismena shook her head furiously, and Isobel pulled back so she could check, making sure all her limbs were intact. Finding nothing physically wrong, she hugged her tightly.

"Is she okay?" Nye asked, appearing at their side. "That was some light show."

Ismena sobbed quietly, burying into Isobel's lap.

"She seems to be fine," she replied. "Just tired and frightened."

"We certainly weren't expecting...that," the spy said, smoothing his palm against the little witch's forehead.

"Where are Reed and Gabby?" Isobel asked, scanning the stone circle. Seeing that Alex and Tristan had fallen to the ground, she said, "Are they..."

"They'll be fine," Nye said, rising to his feet.

"They'll wake up and find out they missed the fireworks. Lucky bastards."

He crossed the clearing and joined Reed, who still held Gabby in his arms. Isobel hid a smile, sensing the vampire had developed a little crush on the witch. How it wasn't obvious to her friend was beyond her.

Gabby stirred, moaning softly as her eyes opened.

"Easy," Reed murmured. "You've got one hell of a bump on your head.

"They're gone," Gabby said breathlessly, trying to push away from him and stand.

"Eleanor?" Reed asked, helping the witch to her feet.

She nodded, leaning against the standing stone, her shoulders hunched as she caught her breath. "All of them."

"How do you know?" Nye asked as Reed moved off to check on Alex and Tristan.

"Ismena," she said, glancing at the little witch. "When she tapped into her power, I was somehow connected to her. I was out cold, but I saw everything. The Unhallowed are just...gone. All traces of them... From here... The other side..."

"Shh," Isobel said as much to Gabby as to Ismena. "Are you going to be okay? The shadow..."

"What shadow?" the witch asked with a frown.

"Ismena was desperate to save you from the shadow inside you. That's why we stowed away," Isobel explained. "So? Are you okay?"

Gabby hesitated, thinking before she spoke. "It's always been there, and I've tapped into it before. This time... I'll be okay."

"Hear that, Mena?" she murmured to the little girl in her arms. "Aunt Gabby is going to be okay, thanks to you."

Ismena began to sob softly in her arms. "Mommy, I want to go home."

"Good idea," she replied, smoothing down her matching fiery hair. "Let's go home."

Chapter 20

I sobel and Nye stood side by side on the balcony, watching their daughter in the garden below.

The wilted wasteland had been transformed into a lush oasis of greenery, the lawn a brilliant emerald, and the trees full to bursting with leaves. Considering it was the beginning of December, it was completely unnatural. Ismena had been busy practicing with her powers, by the looks of it. That girl had the greenest thumb she'd ever seen. Needless to say, Alex was pleased his niece took after him.

"Did you get a good one?" Isobel asked.

"Of course, I did." Nye bristled. "What do you take me for?"

"Christmas is no joke," Isobel declared. "The tree is the most important part of the decorating process."

"The tree is fine," he said with a groan. "Its

proportions are symmetrical, and it takes up half the living room."

"Good. It's Mena's first Christmas, so we've got to make it special."

"By allowing a tree to fall on her?"

"Nye, seriously?" Isobel complained. "Have you seen the size of her? She's taller than you."

He rolled his eyes. "Don't remind me. They grow up so fast these days."

"I know, right? Two months old and she's already legal drinking age."

Turning her attention back to their daughter, she laughed as Ismena twirled, her long fiery hair flaring as she brought a shrub to life. Her little girl had transformed into a beautiful, young woman right before her eyes. Their fears about her future seemed to be laid to rest for the time being as she seemed to have stopped growing a few days ago. Just as Gabby had theorised, Mena had grown to maturity, and there she'd remained.

"Did you realise that Reed was Tristan's son?" Isobel asked, thinking about their family. "I had no idea. Not until Gabby told me."

"Neither did I," Nye replied. "Guess the old bastard has something to live for, after all."

"Besides Ismena? He's besotted, you know. She's like a daughter to him."

"As long as it stays like it."

"*Pfft*," Isobel spat. "Do you really think he'd romance her? Unlikely."

"I still have that video of him playing with pink ponies," the spy grumbled. "I'll use it if I have to."

"I always knew you were a big softy," she quipped, jamming her elbow into his stomach.

"As long as you keep it to yourself, we'll have no problems...behind closed doors." He wiggled his eyebrows. "Mena was a one-time occurrence, you know. I'm back to firing blanks."

"Thank, *God*." Isobel laughed, thankful she'd never have to give birth to another magical baby ever again... she hoped.

Nye turned his gaze back to the garden as Gabby appeared on the lawn with Ismena.

"Who knew how long Gabby was carrying around that secret," he mused.

"The dark power she was born with?" Isobel asked. "Knowing her, it was likely years."

"She's fond of sacrifice, but then again, witches are a self-righteous lot."

"Careful, Nye," Isobel said, wrapping her arms around his waist. "Your daughter comes under that umbrella, remember?"

"Who? Mena?" He smiled mischievously. "She's in a class of her own."

"The Immortal Witch," Isobel whispered. "She's going to do some incredible things. I'm sure of it."

"No doubt," he replied, lowering his lips toward hers. "No doubt at all."

Gabby stood on the patio at the Hampstead manor and gazed out over the garden.

Smiling, she watched as Ismena twirled on the lawn and brought a little shrub back to life, its leaves sprouting and forming perfect emerald tips.

Ismena turned once more, her hair fanning out as she went, and finding the older witch watching her, she smiled proudly, pleased as punch with her handiwork. The air shimmered around her as her power coaxed all the flowers in a ten-meter radius into full bloom. Petals unfurled in the thousands, and the sweetest scent filled the air.

Gabby raised an eyebrow but allowed the witch her fun. A thousand roses in bloom wasn't exactly natural for the beginning of winter, especially when the air was full with the promise of snow.

Bundling her hands into her coat pockets, she descended the stairs and joined the witch on the lawn. Ismena had grown so fast they'd had a hard time keeping her clothed, but now that she seemed to have reached maturity, her closet and Isobel's had been thoroughly raided. Mena currently wore an emerald coat belonging to her mother and Gabby's purple woollen hat. Her hair loose around her shoulders, the deep ginger locks reached down her back, almost touching her waist. Gabby had already made sure Nye was banned from teasing his daughter with 'ginger ninja' jokes.

Mena was a beauty—that was for sure. She was the image of her father with the spirit of her mother.

"Aunt Gabby," she said. "How did I do?"

"Hmm," she murmured, looking over the garden. "All these plants are out of season, but they're formed perfectly. But you already knew that."

"Then we shall save them until spring." Ismena laughed and waved her hand. At her command, the flowers curled in on themselves, closing back into tiny little buds. All but a single brilliant red rose on the bush before them.

"I still don't understand what you did that day," Gabby said, kneeling down and smelling the bright bloom. Its sweet scent filled her nose, and she smiled. *Impeccable.*

"If I'd let you tap into your dark power to face Eleanor, she would've forced you to become like her."

Gabby rose to her feet and glanced at the witch. "You're saying it was a trap?"

Ismena nodded. "There was no other way."

"There's always another way," she said stubbornly.

Ismena placed her hand on Gabby's shoulder and smiled. "I don't blame you, Aunt. I know you believe you betrayed me by allowing me to use my power against Eleanor, but it's all right. It was what I was meant to do."

"You were just a little girl. None of us wanted you to grow up thinking you were only with us because of your abilities."

"I never was," she said. "I'm with you because you love me despite the reason I was created. All of you."

"Mena! Come inside!"

She glanced back at the house at the sound of Isobel's voice and smiled.

"Are you coming?" she asked Gabby. "Tristan's told me all about Christmas, and I'm very excited. Dad has brought us a tree to decorate. Will you help?"

"Only if you don't cheat and use your powers."

"Of course, not. 'The pleasure is in the work, not the result,'" she said, quoting Gabby's words back to her.

"Mena!" came Isobel's voice again.

"You had better go in," Gabby said.

Ismena turned and began to cross the lawn. When she realised Gabby wasn't following, she stopped. "Are you coming?"

The witch nodded and waved her inside. "In a minute, okay?"

Mena glanced at the olive tree and smiled knowingly before making her way inside. Through the kitchen windows, Gabby caught sight of Isobel embracing the witch before they disappeared deeper into the mansion.

Turning to the olive tree, she smiled. "Well, Regulus?" she asked. "How did I do?"

A cold droplet of ice settled on her nose, and she shook her head. Another flake fell before her, and she glanced up at the sky as the first snow of the season began to fall, softly at first, then heavier, coating the garden with a blanket of shimmering white.

Laughing, she glanced at the olive tree one last time, and then went inside to join the others. Reed would be waiting for her under the mistletoe, and there was no way she was missing that.

Somewhere on the other side, she knew Regulus was looking down on them, smiling at the irony and uttering the words, "Not half bad...for a witch."

Want more novels just like this one? Check out Nicole's other series:

AUSTRALIAN SUPERNATURAL - In the harsh and unforgiving Australian Outback lies the tiny opal mining town of Solace. A witch runs the general store, a vampire cuts and polishes opal, the mechanic is a werewolf, a fae is the local layabout, and an elemental works the mine. But what's hidden underneath the baked earth is the most dangerous thing of all.

THE ARONDIGHT CODEX - An ancient war with demons. A lost sword with the power to end it all. And a woman with purple hair is the world's only hope.

THE CAMELOT ARCHIVE - Set in the same alternate Arthurian world seen in **The Arondight Codex**... Deadly secrets. Murder and revenge. The end of the world is nye and Camelot is the last bastion of hope.

THE WITCH HUNTER SAGA - Vampires and witches collide in this thrilling Urban Fantasy adventure. You've never met vampires quite like these...

THE CRESCENT WITCH CHRONICLES - Witches, shapeshifters, and ancient myth collide in this colourful Irish flavoured series! Come on an adventure fraught with danger and forbidden romance... and the ultimate battle to save magic before it's gone forever.

THE DARKLAND DRUIDS - A woman with no living relatives travels from Australia to the other side of the world to find out the truth of who she is...only to land in the middle of a prophecy of destruction. Druids, witches, fae, and shapeshifters abound in this thrilling magical adventure!

Find out more at: NicoleRTaylorWrites.com

See what titles are FREE at: Nicole's Free Reads

ABOUT NICOLE

Nicole R. Taylor is the author of the bestselling Urban Fantasy series, The Witch Hunter Saga.

She writes about vampires with complexes, insane witches, super heroes, post-apocalyptic warriors and samurai sword wielding women...all from a desk in a country town near Melbourne, Australia.

Follow Nicole Online:

Website: www.nicolertaylorwrites.com
Twitter: twitter.com/nicole_noir
Facebook: facebook.com/nrtaylorwrites
Newsletter: www.nicolertaylorwrites.com/newsletter
Email: nicole.this.is@gmail.com

www.ingramcontent.com/pod-product-compliance
Lightning Source LLC
Chambersburg PA
CBHW060812190726
48285CB00002B/636